MARIE'S
WATCH

REBECCA L. MATTHEWS

TATE PUBLISHING
AND ENTERPRISES, LLC

Published by Tate Publishing & Enterprises, LLC
127 E. Trade Center Terrace | Mustang, Oklahoma 73064 USA
1.888.361.9473 | www.tatepublishing.com

Tate Publishing is committed to excellence in the publishing industry. The company reflects the philosophy established by the founders, based on Psalm 68:11,
"The Lord gave the word and great was the company of those who published it."

Book design copyright © 2014 by Tate Publishing, LLC. All rights reserved.
Cover design by Arjay Grecia
Interior design by Caypeeline Casas

Published in the United States of America

ISBN: 978-1-62902-960-3
1. Fiction / Christian / Historical
2. Fiction / General
13.11.26

DEDICATION

With pleasure, I dedicate this story to Dick and Roberta, who are living examples of God's unconditional love. I've been blessed beyond measure by knowing them and witnessing their faith as they consistently seek, trust, and obey God's will in their lives.

CHAPTER

1

She gazed around at the breathtaking scene; a smile played on her lips. The ladies were dressed in beautiful gowns, and the gentlemen looked dashing in their suits. The musicians performed as couples danced. The fashion worn at this class reunion denoted an era long past. Festive lights twinkled from where they dangled above the crowd.

The infectious sounds of laughter and the clinking of glasses held high by reunited friends wrapped Marie in a sea of joyful elation. Streamers adorned the large hall, candles flickered within frosty chimneys at each table, and the food buffet, which flanked the entirety of one large wall, was being tended by a crew of neatly uniformed caterers. The aromas of roast turkey and ham wafted about the room with each slice of the carver's knife.

The five-piece band beckoned many to the tiled dance floor. The colored gowns swirled and swayed, at times engulfing the stark-black contrast of their partners' suits. Small groups gathered in a few locations within the large room, and tables were peppered with others choosing to dine while they conversed.

"I'm glad you came. It's nice to see you again," Marie said to a woman who was passing by. "It's been a long time."

The woman paused briefly, but Marie's attention wasn't directed toward her, so she moved on.

Marie was a beautiful woman. She greeted friends she hadn't seen in years. Though she was courteous to the people in attendance, it was clear she was preoccupied. Time and time again, her gaze fell upon the door leading to the entryway.

"Hi! How've you been?"

Marie turned toward a former classmate who had stepped toward her, a man she vaguely remembered. She wasn't quite paying attention, but his questions prodded for answers.

"Yes, I'm married, and we have a daughter." Marie's voice trailed off, and her smile faltered before resuming its place upon her full and rosy lips, though worry tugged at the corners.

Her visitor passed on, noting her indifference.

Marie was wearing a pale yellow gown that was fitted to her petite waist and draped to the floor, giving her the silhouette of a goddess. The capped sleeves became nearly sheer as they tapered to her dainty wrists. Her posture offered nothing less than proper form, and the classy fit of her attire indicated she could have been a woman of wealth and fine upbringing. The milky white complexion of her face, with only a proper hint of color, set the stage for her dramatic, dark eyes to catch one by surprise. She wore her chestnut hair pulled back with a wisp of tendrils left free to frame her face. She was a vision.

This gathering in early June of 1932 was one only the wealthy could afford, and wealth was in short supply ever since the stock market had crashed. The staff was solemn as they wandered among the crowd delivering drinks and offering hors d'oeuvres. They appeared detached and methodical as they worked.

Marie, seeming to remember something of import, strode determinedly through one of the doors to the rear of the great room. Making her way down a corridor and a set of steps, she entered a room where there were children playing, being watched by nannies dressed in uniform. As she perused the room, a young girl about the age of five rushed to wrap her arms around her waist.

"Mommy, you look beautiful."

Marie gazed down at Abigail. "Thank you, darling." Marie's soothing tone brought a smile to her child's face.

Grasping Marie's hand, Abigail pulled her toward the group of rambunctious kids. "Mommy, look who's been my nanny."

An older woman stepped from the crowd of children to greet Marie. "Hello, Mrs. Towell. How are you this evening?" She was well groomed; not a hair strayed from her tight bun. She seemed a bit firm for Marie's taste.

"I'm fine, Miss Sidney. Thank you." It was difficult for Marie to hide her disappointment in the nanny assigned to her daughter this evening. She had cared for Abigail on a number of previous occasions.

"And may I point out how fine you look in that gown," commented Miss Sidney, who very seldom shared opinions. It felt odd to Marie that she offered one now.

"Ma'am, I needed to speak with you. I must be leaving by eight o'clock. I know you've been told, but I wanted to remind you."

Marie glanced at the clock and felt pressed for time. Seven o'clock would be upon them in just more than twenty minutes, and her husband had still not arrived. She bent down to her daughter and kissed her cheek.

"Okay, love. I'm going back to my party but will return with your father by eight."

As Marie rose to her full height of five and a half feet, her daughter grasped her hand in both of hers and tugged to pull her back down. Tiptoeing as high as she could reach, she placed a kiss upon her mother's cheek in return.

"Okay, mommy. See you soon."

Marie glanced back once she reached the door to see her daughter holding hands with Miss Sidney. She pondered her dislike of this woman and wondered what it was that made her feel uneasy. Abigail always seemed happy when she was with

Miss Sidney, yet there was an aura of darkness around the nanny that concerned Marie. Opening the door, she returned to the party upstairs.

CHAPTER

2

Marie was just reaching the lobby when she saw David coming up the stairs. The doorman opened the door for him as Marie rushed to greet him.

"Where've you been? The reunion's been well under way, and our friends have been wondering if you're really coming. I keep telling them what a busy man you are." Marie reached up to embrace her tall husband then wrapped her arm through his.

"Just now I was able to get away from the office. I'm sorry if I've kept you waiting. I didn't know there was a reunion taking place tonight. Please forgive me." He smiled down at Marie. "How's Abigail? Is she enjoying the festivities?"

"Oh, yes. I think so anyway. Miss Sidney is with her." With a quick glance around, Marie leaned in closer. "You know, I don't much like her. I think she's putting bad ideas into our daughter's head. Perhaps I should have her replaced."

Marie became quiet as she considered Miss Sidney's true motives for being with Abigail. She started to feel her heart race and fought the temptation to return to the nursery immediately and retrieve her daughter.

Shaking those thoughts aside, she remembered that time was not in her favor to accomplish all she had hoped this night. She looked up at her husband and asked, "What time is it?"

David pulled his coat sleeve back to see the face of his watch. Marie was feeling anxious as she tried to see it as well. He was taking his time and was too calm. Didn't he realize they had to rush?

"Mm, it's nearly seven. Why? What is it?"

She considered her options. The reunion would have to wait, she decided. Marie turned to the doorman and smiled before grabbing her husband by the hand.

She glanced at David with a crafty look. "Come, let's be quick."

Not giving the doorman the opportunity to do his job, she opened the door herself, pulled her ball gown up within her free hand, and tugged David into a trot as they raced down the marble stairs and across the parking lot. Reaching the grass, she continued her explanation but did not slow her pace.

"Miss Sidney, she has to leave by eight. There's not much time." She cast a flirting look at her husband, which brought a similar smile to his face.

They arrived at the neighboring apartment building in minutes where the doorman smiled, tipped his hat, and held the door open for the familiar couple. They breezed past and entered the well-maintained lobby. It was old, which offered a character that was desirable, and it was located in the heart of Raleigh, which gave additional value. It was centrally located to the most influential of businesses as well as the capitol building.

The community of leaseholders who rented these accommodations did not know one another. In most cases the comings and goings of each tenant was private, which is why they chose this building. The security was first rate, and that was reflected in the price.

David and Marie entered the elevator. She giggled and, releasing her husband's hand, pushed the button that would lead them to her destination. David smiled when she looked back at him. She loved him so much.

"I love you, Marie." His voice was soft.

Marie smiled in response. He was a devoted husband. She often felt like she didn't deserve him. She was blessed.

"Thanks. I love you, too." She felt the heat rise to her cheeks, but she needed to pay attention now. She glanced up and focused on the numbers as they ascended floor by floor and waited for just the right moment before stating, "Here we are!"

Whether it was an obsession, or some oddity, she had to announce their arrival just before the bell rang. It was a game that took all of her attention, but she rarely missed her cue.

The elevator opened to a comfortably furnished and extremely neat apartment. It was the best. The view was stunning, especially from the balcony. The neighborhoods of the city were below, and the clear sky of this warm June night spread out above. Though nights like this didn't happen often, Marie loved when she was able to be home with David.

"What time is it, David?" Marie's voice was rushed, and though she was smiling, she knew the concern could be heard in her voice.

After a glance at his watch, he responded, "It's just after seven."

She felt the pressure of time. "Oh no, come. We must hurry." Marie pulled him through the apartment to the doorway of his bedroom. "There's not much time. Here, help me with this, please." She turned her back to him and held her head to the side as David unzipped the back of her gown. She watched the look on his face.

Shrugging out of the sleeves, she dropped it to the floor and climbed onto the four-poster bed. "Come, honey." She smiled and patted the space beside her.

He answered her urgency, undressed, and slid onto the bed beside his wife.

CHAPTER

3

"It's nearly eight o'clock, Mr. Towell." Miss Sidney sounded irritated when David and Marie arrived to claim their daughter.

"I'm aware of that, Miss Sidney," David responded in an equally firm voice.

"Daddy! Daddy!" Abigail stood quickly from the puzzle she was working on in the corner of the room. She ran to David as he knelt and snuggled into his embrace.

"Daddy, Miss Sidney was helping me make that puzzle. Isn't it beautiful?" she asked, stepping back. Abigail pulled at David's hand. "Come see."

"Mr. Towell, I must leave now."

"Yes, Miss Sidney. We're leaving." David turned his attention back to his daughter and followed her lead. "Honey, that's beautiful. Good job. I'm proud of you."

Abigail looked up at her dad's face and smiled.

"Honey, we have to clean it up now."

"Oh, I don't want to break it. I'm not done." Abigail looked pleadingly at her father.

"Mr. Towell, I must leave," Miss Sidney's sharp voice broke in.

Abigail ran to her. "Please, Miss Sidney. Can I leave it?" Her voice was shaky. "We can work on it again, can't we?"

Miss Sidney looked down at her. "Miss Abigail, you know the rule about cleaning up each night." Returning her attention to the parents, Miss Sidney continued, "I must really leave now."

"Thank you for your help with our daughter," David said. "Come on, honey."

David helped Abigail take the puzzle apart and put it away. He then took Abigail's hand and placed an arm behind his wife as they exited the nursery together.

"Abigail, I'm proud of you for following the rules without complaining. I know that was hard."

Abigail turned her attention to her father as they went up the stairs. "It's okay. We're busy tomorrow anyway."

Then she whispered, "'Cause it's gonna be my birthday." She looked up at her daddy, and he gave her a wink. "Daddy, how was your day? I missed you."

"Thanks, honey. I had a busy day, but I'm glad to be with you. Sorry I'm so late."

"Don't you think Mommy looks pretty?"

David turned toward Marie and smiled. "Yes, honey. I think she's radiant."

"Radiant? What's that?" Abigail laughed.

"Very beautiful, honey. I think she's very beautiful." David paused and kissed his wife. "And her beauty shines like the sun."

"Come on, Mommy and Daddy." Abigail giggled and pulled at her parents to move them forward.

The trio entered the great room where Marie had been waiting for her husband earlier. Gone were the decorations that had adorned the halls, gone were the musicians and gaily clad dancing couples, and gone was the very memory that had consumed Marie's mind and caused her to dress tonight in such grand fashion.

The staff was present, just as they were earlier, and so were the patients they tended in this high-class transition house, a transition house for the mentally ill.

The Towell family settled into an intimate seating arrangement off to one side of the great room, not an uncommon sight to those who worked here. Abigail played at her parents' feet, setting up an imaginary tea set on the coffee table. David spoke with his wife and daughter. He also watched at times as they talked to seemingly no one at all.

After an hour of visiting, David leaned forward and kissed his wife. "Honey, I'm sorry, but we have to leave now. It's getting late for Abigail. We'll see you in the morning."

"Mommy, it's my birthday tomorrow," Abigail said excitedly.

David expected that she had repeated those words a million times throughout the day.

"Really, Abigail, that's very exciting," Marie responded, sounding like she cared but didn't really understand.

David kissed his wife goodnight then walked to the door holding hands with Abigail. He shook his head and laughed as he realized how much he loved the bizarreness of his life. With God in control, every day was a surprise.

David looked back as one of the nurses approached his wife. Their lives were drastically different than most, but there was so much love.

David took his daughter next door to their plush apartment and settled her in to bed before retiring for the night himself in the bed he and his wife had occupied only a couple hours earlier. He held her in his prayers and thanked the Lord for the love they shared regardless of the illness he had allowed in their lives.

CHAPTER

4

David's wife had begun showing signs of odd behavior when their daughter was three years old. At the age of twenty-two, Marie had been proving herself a wonderful homemaker, mother, and wife, but something was just not right; David could tell. He worried that her time home alone for long periods of time without him were causing her to feel lonely. In the beginning he thought the quiet chatting to herself was her way of working through worries, or perhaps she was keeping herself company. Though, when prodded, she denied these conversations were taking place, almost defensively.

Marie had married young to David, a much older man. As a seventeen-year-old bride, she had been swept off her feet by this handsome thirty-year-old businessman. David's home life as a child had left much to be desired. He had a terribly harsh father and a mother who seemed indifferent and timid. They did not work well together, and the uncomfortable atmosphere was unhealthy for a growing boy. As a child he spent most of his time alone, reading and planning great adventures.

When David was older his great adventures led him to form stable businesses, which he sold once he felt all quirks were ironed out and they were thriving. He became known as a person to watch. Investors watched his ideas grow, each vying for the attention of this talented man.

For someone uncomfortable with people, David attracted a lot of attention. He preferred the silent businessmen who were straightforward in their offers to those who fawned for attention.

Numbers were his thing. When he was young he could play out scenarios in his mind mathematically, like a game, such as the population of coons versus the potential demand for coon dogs necessary to hunt them. He calculated based on information he would gather by way of conversations overheard at the mercantile in the village. When he was nine he had saved up pennies from birthdays and doing chores for neighbors and bought himself a female blue tick coon dog to breed. He knew that was a sound investment, because the coons were plentiful, and their hides were starting to be in demand. Of course, such a venture would have been foolish if either the supply or demand hadn't been present.

By the time he had finished his schooling, he had saved up a lot of money from little ventures like this that he had pursued. In his late teens he moved out to create a business he was confident would generate its own growth simply by the desire of those who heard of it. David played the game of supply and demand. All the hard work, the fine-tuning, the figuring—it all brought fulfillment to his heart and comfort to his pocket.

David left the village of Wentworth, North Carolina, behind. He was happy to be away from the tense atmosphere of his parents' home. Living alone could only be so much more pleasant, he thought. He purchased a run-down, one room shack three towns north and just over the border in Danville, Virginia, in a state that had yet to declare prohibition. This, David thought, would be the perfect place to launch Stills and Casks, a one-stop location for all things alcohol related. Being on the border of North Carolina, a state steeped deep in "cleansing from the liquid demon," David was sure he would make a lot of money.

Using the loft as his bedroom and office, though the quarters were tight, David transformed that one-room shack into a small store stocked with supplies for the general population to create their own spirits. There were tin cups lined up nicely on the shelf, a still set up in the front corner by the door, a few kegs stacked to look appealing, as well as bottles, corks, cleaning supplies, and anything else a person might need.

He had met his neighbors and the few businessmen in the small town, shared his enthusiastic plans, and was greeted with matched excitement. He made arrangements with the local blacksmith to help, on a paying basis, fashion more stills as orders arose. He met with local farmers and contracted with them for their hops and barley. The townspeople could sense the benefit this newcomer to town was generating. People did enjoy their liquor. What a great idea to give the option to create one's own at-home liquor, especially during such a tumultuous time in history.

After much research and many failed attempts of his own to create all kinds of liquor, wine, and malt beverages, David decorated the outside of his less-than-desirable establishment and held an opening event.

"Thanks for joining my celebration, John." David turned to the banjo player parked on a rickety old chair in the front dooryard.

"I wouldn'ta missed this 'un for the world, David. Looks like the entire town's turned out to check out whatcha been doin'."

David looked around at all the new people in his life and smiled. Kids were playing tag around the big oak tree, couples were sitting on blankets visiting with their neighbors, and the second of eight kegs was being drained quickly. David stood refilling cups held by future patrons, or at least those he intended to make future patrons.

"It's a good turnout. I've been looking forward to this day for a while now. Glad to see so many have come." He stepped forward to call the attention of those milling around.

"Thank you for coming," David, shy but confident, used the loudest voice he could muster. "I'd like to give you some tips on brewing, distilling, and fermenting if you'd take a seat close by."

He beckoned with his hands, bringing the gentlemen around him to sit on the ground and the few chairs he was able to gather together as he began his well-rehearsed demonstrations.

CHAPTER

5

Stills and Casks was the beginning of bigger business for David. When it grew large enough, and before prohibition's hold loomed too close, he sold it to a couple of foolish investors. In nineteen fifteen this transaction made a young man of twenty-one wealthy. For David, it meant much more; he had helped a struggling town prosper. He liked that feeling. However, this community's growth was born of controversy and rebellion, both the country's as well as his own. He had made money, a lot of it, supporting the disruptive behaviors that divided his parents and had robbed his childhood of peace. The townspeople, for the most part, were very thankful for the growth David brought, but he felt less than fulfilled; his conscience was bothering him.

Due to this, his next business plan was taking shape differently. He returned to his home state of North Carolina to search for the right location and for change within his heart. He met with locals, businessmen and women, visited churches, which was something new to him, and perused available properties in many towns. He wanted to be sure the community in which he settled next was right for his hopes and dreams.

After researching locations, travel patterns, ill-kept properties, and under-privileged communities, he found what he was looking for. On the outskirts of a small town called Roxboro, he discovered a large, empty barn on a hundred acres of overgrown farmland where it appeared the farmhouse had burned some time earlier.

The local barber in this small, empty-feeling town had lots to talk about when David stopped in for a trim.

"Well, you're a stranger to these parts. Where do you come from?" the old man asked as he waited for David to sit in his barber's chair. He snapped the cape open and held it as it draped into place around the front of David's tall frame. "Pretty snazzy dresser too, I might add."

David smiled up at the aging gentleman. "I left North Carolina years ago. I'm looking to move back. I thought I'd check out your town."

"Oh, it'd be nice to see some young feller like yerself move into these here parts, but I'm not quite sure this is the place yer lookin' fer." The portly barber turned to grab his scissors and comb then turned back to look at David's reflection in the mirror. "Things haven't been quite right here in years."

"What do you mean? It's a beautiful area." David watched the gentleman's facial expression cloud over a bit as his hand hesitated above David's head with the comb.

"Well, there was an accident some time ago, and it's kinda brought a deep sadness, like a dark cloud, over the whole lot of us."

David watched as the barber became quiet and focused on his haircut as if it was the most important thing at that moment, but David could tell his mind was a million miles away.

"What's your name?" David asked.

The barber snapped his attention back to the present and smiled. "Theodore's my given name, but everyone calls me Teddy. I like that, I guess, seems kinda comfortable, fer a name I mean. What's yer name?"

David smiled; he liked Teddy. "My name's David, David Towell." David released his hand from under the cape and extended it. "Nice to meet you, Teddy."

Teddy shook his hand, then dropped his back to his side, and squinted as he looked at David's reflection. Stepping in front of him, he turned to look him in the face. "David Towell, huh? Seems as I've heard that name somewhere before. Hmm, David Towell."

Teddy resumed his snipping movements with a puzzled look on his face as if determined to figure out this riddle.

"I've been looking for property and took a look at that barn just up the way a bit. You know the one? It has about a hundred acres with it."

"David Towell, David Towell, now where've I heard that name before?" Teddy was mumbling and obviously not paying attention to the discussion David was trying to have.

"Teddy. Do you know anything about that property for sale up the road a bit, the big barn? I walked around it. Seems there was a house there at one time, but it's gone now. Looks like it burned down."

Now that caught Teddy's attention. "No, no, no. You don't want that land. That property's laced."

"Laced? What does that mean?"

"Kinda, um, like a curse. It's laced with sadness. It has the whole town laced in with it. Downright heartbreaking what took place there."

"I really like the property, though. The location, the barn, I really think I can do something with it. It might help this town."

"Uh, I don't think so. I definitely don't think you wanna be there. That's where the sadness came from. It'll git you too. No, you'd do better to steer clear of these parts if you know what's good fer you."

"Come on, Teddy. It can't be that bad. Have some hope. I've got some great ideas, and that property is just begging me to try them out there."

Teddy finished his snipping and untied the cape from David's neck. He brushed away the remnants of hair then took a seat at a small table by the window, pushing the checkerboard aside. He took a deep breath. "David Towell, it was a tragedy, I tell ya. It's difficult to talk about. Nobody ever does anymore, you see, but I know everyone keeps it in their minds."

David turned the barber's chair to face Teddy directly. "Can you tell me? Help me to understand, then maybe I can help it get better."

"Get better? I don't think so." Teddy hesitated, as if he was getting his nerve up. "It were a dark night, no moon, and chilly as late December can git. It was two nights afore Christmas, and we, the whole town, got together at church to celebrate. We weren't a large group, but we was real close-knit-like. The couple that owned that farm was Grant and Mary Spears." Teddy pointed in the direction of the vacant property. "The farm you want to buy, that was the grandest farm in the whole region. They rode home in their new high-wheeler that night. They had much to feel blessed about. They finally, only two weeks earlier, born their first boy, and their farm was gittin' big. Fer a young guy he sure was successful. He was a hard worker."

David wondered if he was detecting tears in Teddy's eyes.

Teddy rubbed his nose then resumed his story. "The four little girls tumbled into the car around Mary and Grant and thems baby brother. I still remember hearin' the Christmas carols they was singin' as they drove away from the church, they was singin' real loud. They was happy." The smile that memory brought to Teddy's lips was replaced by a stern look. "Grant couldn't help 'em, but Mary, she tried. I know she tried." Teddy got quiet.

David broke the silence, "I'm sorry, Teddy. I see how upset this is making you."

Hauntingly, Teddy continued, "It was the fire that caught our 'tention, hours after we left the church. It was too late, then. The sky was blazin' red like the most beautiful sunset. 'Cept it weren't no sunset at all, it was thems house on fire." Teddy looked out the window, his eyes vacant and empty.

"The children, Teddy, were the children in the house?" David asked.

Turning his empty look back to face David, Teddy continued, "When we got there the house was all fallin' in on itself. Just like a log in the fireplace, it all just was fallin' in. The children was in it."

David saw the tears slip down Teddy's plump cheeks now. He waited patiently, feeling it was important to learn the truth about this property.

Teddy took a deep, shuddered breath and continued, "I found Grant in the barn. He was caught in this new, fancy piece of farmin' equipment they'd just got. I could see the blood. There was a lot of it. I ran to him to help, but he weren't breathing. He'd been dead for a while."

"And Mary? What about his wife?" David prodded.

"She was alive when we found her. She was huddled in a corner of the barn near where I found her husband. She had burns all over, real bad ones, her hands and feet was the worst. It was cold out. Her nightdress was all she had on, and that was all burnt and stuck to her arms and legs. She musta tried hard to save her babies. She probably couldn't understand what kept Grant from helpin' 'til she found him there just like I did, dead."

Teddy put his face in his hands and remained quiet for a long moment. When he spoke next it was from the shelter of his hands. "She never said a word. She didn't live through the night."

David dropped his head. He felt the anguish himself for the terrible loss. The loss this young mother and wife must have experienced; the loss of a vibrant, growing and loved family to this community.

David got up and walked to Teddy's side, placing a hand on his bent shoulder. "Thank you for telling me. I know this's been difficult for you to talk about. I'm very sorry."

Teddy stood and offered his hand once more as David covered it with both of his own. "It was nice to meet you, Mr. Towell.

Now you can understand why this is not the place fer you. You're too young to be laced with the sadness we're livin' with."

"Teddy, I'm staying in town tonight. I'll stop and see you tomorrow, if that's okay."

Teddy smiled, and the spell of darkness, for the moment, lifted. "Mr. Towell, I look forward to seeing you again."

The pair walked out the door, and David waved good-bye as he stepped off the porch and walked up the road toward the hundred-acre farm.

CHAPTER

6

This terrible story pulled at David. He wandered the hundred-acre property deep in thought, trekking up a large hill that must have supported the hooves of many cows and hogs in its time. He stopped at the foot of an oak tree at the crest of the hill and sat. As he looked out over the land, he wanted to be sure this was the right choice, not only for himself, but also for this desperately hurting community.

It came to mind to pray to God, someone he had never conversed with before. The oddity of the thought hung with him for a minute. After the sale of Stills and Casks, he was feeling ready for change; his conscience had really bothered him. That business could not possibly survive the prohibition movement, but he knew there were people willing to pay a lot of money in support of rebellion, and he was the beneficiary of that.

Also, he had to admit, there was a welcoming atmosphere at the churches he had been frequenting. Though his attendance had been business focused, the sermons made sense to him. David wondered what was happening in his heart and if God was the one pulling at him.

"Lord, I've not come to you in the past, but it seems only right to ask for your guidance now. Please help these people heal. I can only imagine the hurt they've felt. I pray you can help them laugh again." David thought back to his visit at the church in town and understood why it was nearly empty and lacked joy. "Should I buy this land? Is this where I should invest that money? I'm seeking your wisdom, Lord. Amen."

David wandered back down the hillside and approached the barn. He had walked this property twice before, but now it seemed different, personal. He glanced over to the house's foundation overgrown with vines and shrubs, and closed his eyes. Taking a deep breath, he envisioned the tragedy as it perhaps had unfolded that wicked Christmastime many years before. Tears stung his eyes as he opened them and pulled the barn door open. It was empty now, but he knew it had been the center of growth, excitement, and joy for not only a family, but also a hopeful town, at one time.

Stepping into the center of the vast space, David raised his face upward. "Lord, this problem is too big for me. You're the mighty healer. I heard that just the other day, in the Roxboro Baptist Church, right here in this town."

Just then a loud wailing pierced the air, startling David. He turned and looked but saw nothing, yet the desperate cries continued. It sounded like a baby, and for a moment David thought he was hearing things, conjuring up sounds, possibly evoking a curse from the past. It sounded like an infant in pain, a baby close by in peril. David ran in the direction he thought the sound was coming from.

When he opened a small door at the back of the barn and stepped into a run-down chicken coop, the sound became louder. He glanced about for a baby. The story was so fresh in his mind that he failed to realize the obvious. David pushed at the outer coop door, but it stuck. The crying was loud, just beyond it, beckoning David to push harder.

Suddenly it gave, and as it fell from its hinges, David fell forward into the sunshine and found himself face to face with a young dog that had cornered a rabbit.

As the dog shied away, yelping in surprise, the rabbit took full opportunity of the situation. David watched as it darted here and there, leaping in graceful bounds until it disappeared down a hole under the stone foundation of the old farmhouse.

"Got a second chance, huh, rabbit?" David's gaze left the spot the rabbit had disappeared and settled on the dog peering around the corner of the barn. "That was eerie. I could've sworn it was a baby. It's not like I haven't heard a rabbit cry before."

David chuckled and shook his head as he rose from the ground. Feeling pain in his leg, he realized he had hurt his knee in the process of falling. As he lifted his pant leg to view his wound, he caught sight of the dog pacing nervously at a distance.

David could tell the pup was a stray. It was skinny and dirty and seemed awfully young. He opted to ignore the dog and took a seat where he could lean against the barn wall. He began whistling softly and glanced over to see the dog creeping closer.

"Here, buddy. It's okay." David used a quiet voice, but the dog stopped at the sound of it.

It scurried back, appearing cautious when David turned his head to face it directly. It seemed caught between curiosity and fear. David remembered a piece of jerky he had put in his pocket earlier and slowly reached down. After a moment, he brought the dark brown piece of meat out and waved it a bit in the air, hoping to entice the pup. If he was a stray, he was probably hungry, and just the scent of food might overrule the fear.

"Come on. It's okay." David's voice was soothing, and he watched from the corner of his eye as the dog crept closer. He kept the jerky in his hand but lay his hand on his lap.

The dog started pacing a safe distance to his left.

David thought back to the rabbit. "Second chance, huh?" Suddenly he sat up straighter, startling the dog again. "Wait a minute. You got a second chance. That's it. It was a sign!" A smile spread on his face, and he settled once more against the barn wall to await the expected approach of this skittish dog. "Lord, that was a quick answer. Thank you." David nodded ever so slightly. "Yeah, it feels right to me too."

After half an hour of patience, the small, tan-and-white, rather unattractive mutt brushed his nose against David's hand as it sniffed the jerky. David waited, and once he felt the inevitable nibble, he held tight to the morsel. The dog's stomach overruled its feelings of caution, and when David reached with his free hand to rub behind its ears, though it cowered ever so slightly, it stayed attentive to the piece of food.

The dog became comfortable with David's touch, and eventually he released the jerky and let him gobble it up before he nuzzled his hand again, looking for more. David smiled and reached up to ruffle its fur with no enticement necessary.

"I think you need a name. Chance, how's that? Chance, I like it."

David rose, and as he walked back into the barn, Chance followed. With new conviction, and a companion at his side, he perused the dimensions of the barn with intent. He had dreamed of this for a long time, and the picture he had developed in his head fit what was in front of him quite nicely.

He wanted laughter to fill these walls. A large lodge filled with families on vacation, playing shuffle board, dancing, dining, swimming; there was so much David felt he could provide to offer an amazing vacation experience. He envisioned a large dining room so guests could feel they were part of a bigger family, a library with dark mahogany walls to lend an atmosphere of serenity, a ballroom to hold the grandest of balls—all this and more.

Though the old building would need to be reinforced, keeping the original structure intact would look great, David thought. The land and its small pond were perfect for horseback rides, a small petting farm, and hunting parties; every season could be embraced.

Now David needed to share his idea with the townspeople. A business such as this would change what they had become used to. He wanted to help, not hurt. Since receiving the sign from above, confidence filled him. He would begin the conversation with his new neighbors in the morning. He headed back to town to a room he had rented above the small general store.

When he settled in for the night, he sat down on the floor beside a bowl of water he had set out for Chance and shared the rest of his jerky and the couple of rolls he had brought for dinner.

CHAPTER

7

"David Towell, how are you?" Teddy smiled and clapped David on the back as he stepped through the door of the barbershop.

There were three other men in the room, one seated in the barber's chair and two playing checkers. All glanced up as David stepped in.

"I'm good, Teddy. How are you?"

"Good, good. Looks like ya got yerself some company." Teddy pointed to Chance, who had settled down on the porch just outside the doorway.

David glanced back at the dog. "Yeah, have you seen him before?"

"Can't say's I have. You guys?" Teddy asked his patrons, who all shook their heads.

"Got yerself a dog, do ya now?"

"I guess so. I found him at that property I'm looking to buy."

Teddy shook his head. "Still considerin' that?" He lowered his voice a bit, looked about the room, and added, "Even after I told ya 'bout the accident?"

"I feel even stronger about it now because of that. I want to share my plans with folks to see if the town would be willing to support me. I mean, maybe, due to the sadness and all, maybe you don't really want a stranger coming in and changing things." This got the attention of the men in the room. "But I think I can help."

"What kind of change you talkin''bout, mister?" the man who had been shuffling the black checkers around spoke up. He was wearing faded overalls and a plaid shirt. He must have been nearly sixty, David guessed, and his hair was all askew. David wondered if he was waiting his turn for the barber's chair; it looked like he needed it.

Directing his attention to the man who had just spoken, David continued, "I have lots to talk about with everyone. I want people to ask questions, share their thoughts and concerns. I want the town on board with what I'm hoping to do. I think it'll be helpful here." David looked around at the others in the room. "I want to hold a meeting and invite all who'd like to attend."

David turned to Teddy. "Do you know who I should talk to? I figure the best place to hold this meeting would be in the church. What do you think, Teddy?"

"Pastor Dean, he'd be the one, and you can find him there at the church. He can get the word out fer ya. Can ya share a bit with us now?"

"I'd love to, Teddy, but I really want everyone to hear all at once. I'm sure you understand."

David reached out to each man, shaking their hands as he left, and walked a block to the church, leaving the chatter he was sure was taking place behind him.

———⁓◦◦◦◦◦◦⁓———

The church was packed. People filled the pews, and the walls were lined with those left standing. The back of the church held even more crowding in shoulder to shoulder. Flyers had been posted, and rumors had spread that the old Spears Farm was likely going to be bought. Everyone wanted to hear what this stranger's intentions were. The atmosphere held concern; the sadness was strong, yet there was a hint of excitement in the air, an excitement not felt since before the Spears family had passed.

Pastor Dean approached the pulpit and, raising his hands, urged everyone to be quiet. A hush fell across the crowd.

"Now, people, as you've heard, we're having this gathering to learn about some possible changes to our town. I understand this person is hoping to purchase the Spears Farm, and he'd like to tell you his plans."

Murmurs rolled through the group.

He raised his hands once more for quiet. "I'd like to introduce David Towell."

The room hushed as David replaced the pastor at the pulpit. "Hi, my name's David Towell. I recently sold a business in Virginia, and I'm interested in investing the profits here in Roxboro. I began Stills and Casks in a small town much like yours, Danville grew a lot due to that business."

At the mention of his former business, the crowd began to mutter loudly.

David continued, "It was a business that was welcomed by the townspeople, and with their support, it helped to transform their small community into a busy town, offering them opportunities they'd not previously had."

David looked at his audience and had to raise his voice over the tone of anger that was growing. He knew this Baptist community would be hard pressed to support someone who neglected the push for prohibition so blatantly. "I enjoyed helping that community. They did benefit from the changes my business brought."

"Evil changes!" The man who spoke stood and looked around, seeking support.

David waited quietly as the crowd settled a bit. He prayed for the right words. He could sense a miracle would be necessary at this point. "I understand your discomfort and the anger toward someone who didn't support the values held strong here. I ask you to be open, to listen to my hopes, to ask questions, and to offer help if you want. I want to make change that is wholesome and good. I want to bring prosperity to a community that is deserving of it and would appreciate it. I am a businessman. I have something to offer. Listen to my plans."

David shared his hopes and dreams as far as this property was concerned. Most in attendance seemed to hope along with him. He was sure this was what he was seeing in their eyes.

"Times are good in our country. I understand there's been tragedy here, but I'm willing to suggest that a vacation destination will bring happiness, laughter, and prosperity to this town once more."

There were smiles, there were hushed whispers, there was hope, and it was tangible.

"I want you to welcome this opportunity with me. A venture like this will bring change, a lot of it. I only want to bring this opportunity to you if you're ready."

People were nodding now; there were only a scarce few who seemed content to hold on to the sadness that had been draped about their shoulders like a heavy shawl, and a few others focused on the irritation they felt for the man before them. They kept a scowl on their faces but were finding themselves the minority as the evening wore on.

"With the hiring of many in this very room, I'd like to transform that old barn into a beautiful resort. I want the pastures to hold horses. I want the pond to hold swimmers. I want dancing and games. I want people to spend time with loved ones and make memories that will last a lifetime, good and wonderful memories."

The vein of life was palpable. There was something, finally something, to look forward to.

"I want that which has brought sadness and despair to a loving community to offer joy once more." David looked at the eyes of each person within the walls of the church. He felt a connection here that could only have been laid out from above. He was not hesitant to acknowledge it.

"I haven't been a God-fearing man, hadn't given it much thought in the past. Something about this town, about this venture, about that property has brought me into a—" David sought for the right words. "A partnership with God. I feel his hand in all this, and that's something new to me. It's nothing I've ever felt before, but it's strong."

David became quiet as he thought of God's power and love. He then looked back to the crowd. "You've patiently listened to my hopes, now I'd like to hear yours. Please, ask questions, share your thoughts."

The applause was thunderous. The crowd rose as they showed their appreciation for this stranger in their midst. For David the feeling was overwhelming. He had only wanted to invest, to venture on, to share that opportunity with others. He had no idea the impact he was having on a hurting town. They were ready for change, and though there were a few hesitant and a little less than trusting, together they would journey forward.

Teddy spoke up first, "I knew I'd heard yer name." He chuckled. "Yer the guy from Virginia what's been makin' all the news. Yer quite well known in a controversial sorta way. Even so, I'd love to have you help this town."

Applause arose again as neighbor nodded to neighbor, and smiles spread across faces in understanding.

CHAPTER

8

It seemed like a monumental task, but with the townspeople working hard alongside David, the old barn's familiar façade became the outer package that held amazing changes. Two levels were created within its structure. Through the main entrance, the old barn doors, there was an entryway leading to what would soon be the front desk. The ceiling in the check-in area was left high with the old beams exposed, lending a rustic feel as a first impression. The staff would be able to stand behind a wooden counter with soft lighting above.

Once checked in, guests would move into the great room, which, as its name implied, was large. This room would hold balls, concerts, special dinners, and presentations. David had already begun making contacts and booking shows for the expected grand opening in May of 1917. The community members he hired were talented and detailed in their work. At this point, it would be a couple short months before it all became reality.

Located off the great room was an intimate dining room with a kitchen beyond, soon to be outfitted with the most modern appliances that could be bought. David had been working with the people he'd hired for the kitchen. In an effort to offer the best in the culinary field, he sent four local women, all very talented and already good home cooks, to Boston to train, all expenses paid.

Through a set of doors to the left of the dining room was a library. The walls were going to be dark wood, the windows would reach to its ceiling, and the book selection was going to be diverse. David wanted all ages and all interests to benefit. There would be tables set up with chairs to accommodate those who wanted to spend serious time researching, and there would be overstuffed couches with coffee tables laden with the most current newspapers in circulation.

Stepping through a rather discreet doorway, you would find yourself back in the great room, entering just under the grand staircase leading to the suites above. When complete, David expected to offer four suites to accommodate up to eight people each, as well as ten individual rooms able to accommodate four people each. There would be two baths available to share on the second story with an additional one on the first floor.

David had designed an office area large enough to hold small staff meetings when necessary; the door to his office was to the left of the front desk. It was here that he was going over the plans, gearing up for another busy day of construction.

"Hey, boss." Scott Tudor knocked, then shot his head around the door without waiting for any response.

Scott was older than David by five years and had lived in Roxboro since he was a small child. He had helped his father build most of the houses that were in town and, after introducing himself to David at the church meeting, quickly became his right-hand man.

David smiled in greeting. "Hi, Scott." He watched him reach down and rub Chance's head. "How was your night? Did the party go well?"

Scott's daughter had turned nine the day before, and his wife had planned a surprise party. Scott brought her to work after school so his wife could get it ready.

"It was good. The party was a surprise to her. She's shy and doesn't really have school friends so it was just family. The look on her face was priceless when she saw my parents." Scott chuckled. "They'd moved closer to Raleigh a few years back so my father could get help for his hurting back. He seems frail. It's strange to see the people you love age. Kind of sad, but it was nice to spend time with them. Thanks for letting me bring her to work. It helped a lot."

"Not a problem. It was nice to see you two together. You seem close. Is she your only child?"

"She is. Unfortunately we haven't been able to have any more. I'm determined to make our relationship the best. She's a great kid." Scott grabbed his carpenter's belt off the floor in the corner and looked at the plans for a minute. "Well, I'm heading off to get something done. Your business isn't going to open on time if you keep me chatting."

Scott laughed as he ducked back out the door, leaving David alone and deep in thought. David had never been very close to his parents, and he was an only child too. It was as if they wished they hadn't had him. Between their fights and the distance they kept from him, he'd felt lonely all of his childhood. He wasn't missing them. That brought a feeling of sadness, an ache, almost a jealousy for what he had missed out on and what others were able to easily share.

I don't understand why that had to be my life. Why, Lord? David's inquiry was simple. An expression of feelings he had repressed all his life.

Pure compassion. The thought came from deep within.

Was that your answer, Lord? Pure compassion? That's not what I got from my parents. Pure compassion. Is that what you feel you've given me by allowing that childhood? That wasn't compassionate. It was difficult.

David felt a wave of anger at God, which shocked him; then he dismissed the thought of his parents, refocusing on the work at hand.

He looked at the plans open before him on the desk. Things were moving along on the construction of the Foxglove Inn. He was happy with the design he and Scott had created and was thankful for such a hard worker at his side. The large group of local workers that joined in the construction was a blessing. He never failed to realize how fortunate he was to be able to employ these people. They seemed appreciative, and it showed in the product they were producing.

David grabbed his carpenter's belt, stepped out of his office and wandered the building, looking at the work in progress and answering the greetings of those that noticed him. He made his way to the kitchen, where he joined the two other men working there. He was not a boss that stood on the sidelines.

CHAPTER

9

After nearly three years of following the Great War overseas, American families were now becoming affected by it. On April 6, 1917, the United States Congress declared war upon the German Empire. Times were changing.

David prayed about the grand opening of the Foxglove Inn that he had scheduled for May 20, 1917. Although the advertisements had already gone out, and the entertainers had already been booked he was feeling sensitive to the declaration and was considering cancelling the event. The following week, though, confirmed the excitement the ads had generated, and the calls to confirm preregistered rooms clearly indicated the grand opening should take place as scheduled. It seemed that with the unrest in the air, there was also the need to take a moment to enjoy something good.

David opted for three different types of entertainment for this special day. In the morning he had scheduled Peter Vondt from Boston, a very talented pianist who would play a wonderful array of music in the great room to add a dimension to the atmosphere as visitors wandered and snacked on brunch-type foods from the trays of strolling waiters.

In the afternoon a choir was scheduled to entertain. They were contracted from the local church. Pastor Dean was excited to have his growing numbers of church members be part of this important event for their town. The choir had been practicing for months, ever since David had approached them prior to Christmas. They had a diverse line-up of songs from somber to festive, taking advantage of this amazing opportunity to challenge themselves and their talents, both individually and as a group.

The evening's schedule was going to be exciting. A popular band, The Triads, were booked as accompaniment for a singing and acting troupe from New York. Under the direction of Fester Court, the guests attending the grand opening of the Foxglove Inn were in for a wonderful evening experience.

The menu was already planned, not only for the day of this event, but also for the following month. For the grand opening there would be food and drinks in constant circulation, as well as meals offered in the dining room at any time of day.

Every room had been booked even prior to the advertisements being published. David Towell was a big name in many circles, and it was expected that something with his name attached was worth the experience.

There were five people hired to work shifts at the front desk. The bellboys had been trained, as had the wait staff, the many groundskeepers, the maids, and the kitchen staff. It felt, at times, as if the entire town of Roxboro was working at the Foxglove Inn. It truly had been a boost to the families, as well as to the town, which had embraced David's hopes and dreams and made them their own.

This once "laced" property was transformed with God's help, and in turn, it now "laced" its happy fingers throughout each life it touched.

David whistled to Chance. He perked his ears and looked at his master.

David held the office door open. "Come on boy."

Chance rose quickly and trotted to the door, where he looked up for further direction.

David stepped into the entryway then out the front doors with his dog at his heels. "Come on, Chance. Let's go for a walk."

David headed around the inn and out to the barn, which was erected on the crest of the hill overlooking the field to the north and the pond to the south. He wanted to check that all was in order. He was expecting a pony, five horses, two goats, two sheep, a dozen chickens, and three bunnies, which were all arriving sporadically throughout the upcoming week. A few of the workers had gotten together and offered to donate some of their animals as tokens of their appreciation. David was grateful.

"Hey, Charlie, how are things looking here?"

Charlie Procter was spreading hay in the waiting stalls of the newly completed barn. "Come see what I've done." Charlie beckoned David into a room beyond the last stall, which was set up as a tack room.

"This looks spectacular. Well done." David offered his hand, which Charlie shook.

"How're things at the inn? It's almost time to open. Do ya think we're ready?" Charlie asked.

"No doubt we're ready. I think the entire country's ready. It seems as though we're going to have quite a turnout," David explained. "I just hope all the excitement doesn't turn to stress. Everyone's trained and should feel comfortable with what they know. I'm comfortable with them."

David sat down on a stool. Chance lay at his feet. He absentmindedly stroked the dog around the ears. "This has been a great experience. When I began I wasn't sure how it would all end up, considering what had happened here. I knew God had a plan, though, and it's been nice seeing everyone, including you, be accepting of the changes."

"You made an impact in our lives." Charlie turned to the tack he had been organizing earlier and reached up to hang a halter. "We're grateful."

"Thanks, Charlie; that means a lot. This community has made me feel at home, a feeling I've never known." David felt a tug of self-pity again for what he never had, those words came to him once more: *pure compassion*. Rising from his seat, he wandered the space, touching the strong-scented leather placed around the room. Saddles, halters, brushes, pails—all the supplies were organized.

"Charlie, you've done well with the spaces out here. This job does suit you."

"Yeah, well, workin' with animals is somethin' I've always enjoyed," he answered.

Charlie was a resident of this small town. Hired by Grant Spears four years before the fire, he had been close to the family and was part of the excitement and growth of the farm. The accident aged him considerably and led him to withdraw. On him, forty-eight looked much older. It took some work just to get Charlie back on the property.

Over time, Charlie had mentioned laughing with the girls and helping around the house as Mary became great with child once more. Grant had not treated him as a hired hand, it seemed, but welcomed him into their lives. They were family to him, and Charlie was part of all their joys, frustrations, excitements, and prosperity. He had given his all to that job and seemed proud to work for a man as fine as Grant Spears. Their deaths were tragic to him.

David felt badly for what Charlie had endured. He was very mindful of what he was asking of him but believed bringing him back to this property and giving him this position was a necessary step in his healing.

CHAPTER

10

David stood in front of the mirror adjusting his black suit, the only one he owned. He bought it to wear at the final celebration he hosted before selling Stills and Casks. He remembered that gathering as he fingered the lapel of his jacket. That party was bittersweet. He had made many acquaintances in Danville, Virginia, but his connection with people, though genuine, was restrained.

David had invested in business for his own gain, but he wanted every investment to also be in community. He wanted others to grow from his decisions. He wanted towns to prosper. He wanted families to have the ability to become stronger. And if a job within a growing company could offer security for one man, then his children might grow up with joy, something David never had.

Returning to the present, David chuckled at the image before him. He was more comfortable in jeans and a t-shirt, they were great inventions. The grand opening was taking place today. The weather was beautiful, and the inn was richly decorated and ready to receive its public.

David bent down to pat Chance, who lifted his head briefly to receive the affection. The personalities of the two could not have been better matched. The more hectic the atmosphere, the calmer they appeared. Chance was comfortable staying in the office for a while as the activity level grew outside the door.

"See you soon, old boy," David mumbled as he opened the door and stepped into the entryway of his newest creation.

"Hey, Mr. Towell."

"Hi, Trisha," David answered.

Trisha smiled at David from behind the front desk as the main door slowly opened, revealing their first guests.

"Here we go," she said as she turned her attention to the man, woman, and three children that appeared to range in age from four to ten.

David turned to greet his guests and offered a hand to the gentleman in front. "Welcome to the Foxglove Inn. I'm David. If there's anything you need, please feel comfortable asking me or any employee of the resort."

The man accepted David's hand and shook it firmly. "Thank you. We're so glad to be here."

"We're happy to have you join us," David responded.

As the two men spoke, the children pushed through to the great room where they stood, open mouthed.

"Mom, Mom! Look at this!"

David turned to see what the excitement was about, realizing it was simply the inn itself.

"This is wonderful," the woman responded as her son grabbed her hand. Turning back to her husband, she said, "Peter, I'm going to take the children over there." She pointed to the large windows, which faced the barn on the hill.

"Excuse me, David. I'm going to check in. It was nice to meet you."

"Certainly. Again, if there's anything we can do, let us know."

The gentleman held his hand out once more. He pumped David's hand even stronger this time as his attention was diverted and drawn in many directions. He stepped away from David and up to the desk.

"Welcome to the Foxglove Inn," he heard Trisha address the man.

David stepped back as he watched this family look around in awe. Having worked daily on the old barn, it had become business, but at this moment, seeing it through the eyes of strangers, he saw it, and a smile spread across his face.

Thank you, Lord, for allowing me this moment. Forgive me for having taken this for granted. David felt God's acceptance in the chills that ran down his spine.

The door opened once more, drawing David's attention to a well-dressed, much older couple.

"Mr. Towell, thank you for inviting us to your grand opening. We've been looking forward to meeting you."

David stepped toward them and shook the hand of Cameron Morrison, a Charlotte lawyer and politician.

"This place is absolutely amazing," his wife said as she looked around with a smile on her face.

"Thank you, and welcome, Mr. and Mrs. Morrison. I do appreciate that. I'm glad you'll be staying," David answered.

"Of course, I want to be one of the first to experience for myself this fantastic inn and all it has to offer." Cameron Morrison smiled and shook his head. "A family vacation resort, what a fantastic idea. Can't wait to see what you'll come up with next. You're quite the businessman," Cameron said.

"Thank you. I guess I enjoy building things. It's been a lot of fun," David answered.

"Building things, that's an understatement. Your business tactics are watched. You're an example to other businessmen around the country, and now"—Governor Morrison waved his hand about the lobby—"people from all over will travel here to spend time in our great state of North Carolina because of you."

"I'm happy you feel this way, and I certainly hope it's as you suggest. That's the goal, after all, to be a destination that draws people. That's success."

"Did you set out to create this when you sold Stills and Casks?" Cameron asked.

David thought for a minute. It seemed so long ago when he first walked this property. It had changed a lot since then. "Yes, I did. In the past I'd focused on what people felt they needed or tapped into their fear of losing something they wanted. This time I wanted to make a difference simply to make a difference."

The door opened behind them as other guests arrived. David and the Morrisons moved out of the way as David continued.

"I knew the type of town I was searching for, one in need of change. This was the right place. When I first stepped foot on the land and saw this big empty barn on acres of rolling hills, I envisioned much of what you see now."

"I like how you work. I'd like to spend time picking your brain while I'm here. Do you think that could happen?"

"Of course." David considered the busyness of the day and, knowing they had reserved their room for two nights, offered a time he hoped would be acceptable. "Would you like to join me before lunch tomorrow in my office?" David pointed to the door at the left of the front desk.

"That would be great. Thank you." Cameron shook David's hand again before stepping forward to check in at the desk.

"Let me introduce you to Trisha," David said. "She'll tell you about your room. I'm going to check on things in the kitchen. Please enjoy your stay, and if you need anything, anything at all, I have confidence that my staff is capable of addressing your needs."

"Thank you, Mr. Towell," Mrs. Morrison said.

Trisha smiled. "Welcome, Mr. and Mrs. Morrison."

David could hear them confirming their arrangements as he stepped away. He glanced through the window and saw three additional motorcars pulling up the drive as he pushed open the door and entered the bustling kitchen.

"Chef, I think we're in for a busy day. How are you feeling?" David walked across the floor, past three ladies who were decorating pastries, and toward Chef Jonathan Howe, who was working his magic at the large New Perfection oil cook stove.

Jonathan Howe had taken the position as head chef, moving from Pennsylvania into a small apartment in town. He was young but eager. Having heard the rumor of this new grand establishment intended to cater up to seventy-two registered guests at a time with more expected for functions, Jonathan showed up while the inn was being built. He introduced himself and asked if the position was available and assured David that, if it was, he was best suited for it. David asked him to stay for a couple of days and help work on the property. He explained that he wanted time to think about it, but in truth, he wanted to observe Jonathan's character and work ethics. He reminded David of himself. He had a vision and took chances to make it happen.

Jonathan turned toward his boss. "Mr. Towell, I'm ready for this opportunity. Thanks to the talented women working with me"—Chef nodded toward the ladies—"I think things'll go smoothly."

"Good to hear, chef." David clapped him on the back. "As you know, there'll be a full house this evening. Are you prepared for the next few days as well?"

"Quite ready, sir. We've prepared salads, some appetizers, and prepped for the next two days' meals, as much as I think is possible. These new refrigerators are fantastic! They'll really help us stay ahead."

David looked over his shoulder at the wall housing the four Kleen-Kold refrigerators. He was sold on the insulating factors and really hoped they would be worth the investment. "Glad to hear. Let me know if there's anything I can do." He turned back toward the women. "Thank you, ladies, for all your hard work."

The three women stopped their work and turned. Sheila smiled and clapped, holding her hands up toward her boss; the others joined her.

"Thank you, Mr. Towell. This has been the best thing that could've happened to me." Sheila looked at her coworkers as they smiled at her. "I think it's fair to say this is the best thing that could've happened to all of us. This is exciting!"

Kelly took a step toward David. "We've been talking about you. What you've done since coming to Roxboro is amazing."

The group nodded.

"We're thankful for what you've done, Mr. Towell."

"It's you I thank." David felt humbled. "This is taking a lot of effort on your part and all the other employees. It's you people that'll make this a success." David turned back to Jonathan. "I'm here if you need anything, chef."

A smile appeared on Jonathan's lips. "Thanks, boss."

David stepped to the door feeling proud of the people God had brought together for this business. There was peace in the air during this very busy time.

CHAPTER

11

As the nighttime entertainment filled the air, David left the crowded inn and walked up to the barn to check on Charlie. Chance had been lying outside on the terrace. David whistled to him. He jumped up and ran on ahead, looking happy as he darted around, chasing scents in the air.

David smiled, remembering his first business, coon dog breeding. It seemed so long ago. Funny how something that seemed insignificant had taught him so much. He learned some business lessons that stuck with him: planning for demand and, in some instances, encouraging that demand to be present. Telling people they need what you're selling goes a long way. Also, people need what someone else has, if you convince a few key people to buy, then you've guaranteed success.

The sun was beginning to set on this beautiful day in May in North Carolina. The fields spread out before him, beckoning to him. He turned from his original course and walked up the hill until it crested, at which point he turned and sat down, looking over the Foxglove Inn. The lights were starting to shine brighter from the windows as the shadows of the day spread. He could hear laughter and music carried on the breeze. A couple was now standing on the terrace, and the shadows of some dancing inside were cast on the lace curtains that covered the French doors.

David watched the couple as they talked. He watched as the woman lifted her head upward and then heard her soft laughter. They hugged and then went back through the doors. Having grown up with so much discontent between his parents, David realized how much it touched his heart to see a couple enjoying each other's company. He had kept his life busy. He supposed this was on purpose. Perhaps he was avoiding something, or someone.

"Lord, what about love? I'm afraid it always turns out bad. I don't want to endure the kind of relationship my parents had. Do you think there's someone for me? Do you think there are relationships where love is kind? If there is, that's what I want." David glanced to the sky and smiled at the beauty of the sunset. There was comfort in that for him. "Well, if so, I look forward to that day."

David stood, brushed off his pants, and whistled to Chance, who broke into a full run for his master. "For now I'm content."

David resumed his walk to the barn and heard a child's voice as he entered. Charlie was handing a young girl hay to feed to a horse that was stretching his head far out of his stall. Scott, his head carpenter, was standing by watching.

David walked up and extended his hand in greeting. "Scott, have you enjoyed your day? You should be proud of the work you've done."

"This has been a life-changing day, I think. Never would I have imagined talking with these politicians or visiting with a famous musician. My wife's having so much fun. It's getting late, though, so I thought I'd bring Marie to say goodnight to the horses before we go home. My wife's getting the last of her dancing in before we go. I'm not much of a dancer."

David looked down at the shy nine-year-old. "Hi, Marie, I don't know if you remember me. I met you when you came to work with your dad one day. It was your birthday, right?"

Her head tilted to look up at David, and she hesitantly nodded. David smiled at her, grabbed some more hay, and handed it to her. Marie smiled in response as she took the hay from his outstretched hand and went back to the horse with it.

Charlie cleared his throat. "Remember to hold yer hand flat, dear. Like this." He held his empty hand open as an example. "Ya wouldn't want ol' Duke to take a bite out of yer hand now, would ya?"

David returned his attention to Scott. "Now that our project's done, do you have anything else lined up?"

"Well, as it turns out, my wife's mother's ill. She lives in northern Pennsylvania. She's been widowed since my wife was about Marie's age. We're going to move in with her so Clara can take care of her. I think I have a good chance of continuing building there, especially since the inn is making news."

David absorbed his words with some sadness. He had gotten close to Scott during their intense nights of planning and many hours of working side by side wielding pencils and hammers. Though most of their time together was quiet and busy, they did share some laughs. David appreciated Scott's personality. He always seemed upbeat.

"Wow, I don't know what to say. I've been absorbed in all we've been doing. It's going to feel different not working together, but even more if you're moving away. Do you think you'll come back?"

Scott nodded. "I'd like to. This is more than just home for me. The work of my father is all around. He was the foundation of who I am as a carpenter. I'm reminded of that daily here. I'm going to miss this area."

"When will you be leaving?" David asked.

"We started packing the house today. I expect to leave by the end of next week."

The two men watched Charlie and Marie in silence for a few minutes. She was patting the horse now. She turned to look at her father. "Daddy, do you think we could have a horse at Grammy's house?"

"I'm not sure, honey. Let's settle in first and see how Grammy's doing."

Marie came to hold Scott's big hand with hers. "Okay, Daddy. Can we find Mommy now?"

"Sure, honey." Scott shook hands with David and then Charlie. "Good night, gentlemen, and congratulations, David, on a spectacular grand opening. I wish you all the best and look forward to returning one day to see how things are going. Perhaps you could use a handyman then."

"You'll always be welcome here, Scott. You're a talented carpenter and a good friend." David turned to face Scott's daughter. "You take care of your daddy, okay?"

She smiled shyly, looking at her father, still holding onto his hand. "I will."

David watched with sadness as his friend slipped through the barn door and into the night. He spoke more to the night than to Charlie. "I sure am going to miss him."

"He's a good man, boss." Charlie's voice drew David's attention.

"Charlie, how was your day?"

"It was a lotta fun. There's a family with three kids that spent so much time up here. They were really good with the animals, too. They want to help me tomorrow. I told 'em they could help feed and water the rabbits."

"That's kind of you to include them."

"It'll be nice to have their help. Like I said, they were good kids. Now if they'd been trouble, I'd have come up with some excuse how I didn't need help." Charlie smiled, causing David to laugh. "How was your day, boss?"

David thought back through the events of the day, the few mix ups, the many smiles, music, and laughter. "Yeah, it was good. Today was memorable." He turned to leave the barn. "It's getting late. You can close down, you know."

"I know, I was gonna a while ago, but I was settin' in the quiet for a minute when Scott came. I'm just gonna make sure every-thin's set for tomorrow. I'll be takin' five people on a trail ride. I already told Chef Jonathan. He's gonna pack a picnic fer us. We'll be gone fer a couple hours."

"Sounds like a great plan." David opened the barn door. "Good night, Charlie."

"Night, boss."

David pondered on his plans for the next day. He was meeting with Cameron Morrison, who'd said he wanted to pick his brain. "Lord, I pray for your guidance. Politics is not for me, but only you know if I have anything to offer. Your will is what I desire. Please guide my words."

CHAPTER

12

In the seven years since the grand opening of the Foxglove Inn, the sleepy little town of Roxboro had grown into a mix of thriving farms and bustling shops. The jazz bands that played every weekend at the inn brought many people from town in to dance. It was a night such as this that David spied a somewhat familiar face in the crowd.

The brown hair had deepened a bit, but the shy smile was recognizable. He felt excited, thinking it meant his good friend Scott was back in town. Taking a chance, he walked up to the young lady, who had just left the dance floor and was getting some punch.

"Marie, is that you?" he asked.

She turned, acting surprised to hear someone call her by name. She smiled in recognition. "Mr. Towell, how nice to see you."

David turned and perused the crowd. "Is your father with you?"

"He's in town with Mother. I asked if I could come dancing."

"When did you get back to town?" David asked excitedly.

"We got back yesterday. Gram died two weeks ago." Marie looked around. "Your inn's doing very well, Mr. Towell."

"It is. I'm sorry to hear about your grandmother, Marie."

"Thanks. She'd been out of sorts, though, the whole time we lived there, as a matter of fact. That's why we moved in with her.

Mom had to take care of her almost like she was a child, but it got really bad in the end. Her passing was a blessing really."

"That must've been tough for all of you."

"It was okay." Marie turned her attention out the back windows. "Mr. Towell, do you think I could go up to the barn? I'd love to see the horses."

"You did seem to like them when you were here before, I remember. Charlie's already gone home, though. I'll take you."

"Are the horses still the same ones you had when you opened?"

"Yes. There's a new one, a colt who was born here a couple years ago. He's quite handsome." David opened the door leading to the terrace and held it for Marie. She had grown up so much. "How old are you now?"

"Sixteen. I'll be graduating school next June."

"Oh my goodness, it's hard to believe how much time has passed."

They walked down the steps and headed up the worn path lined with fragrant flowers as the sun was setting.

"You said your parents are in town. Are you going to move back?"

"We have. They're unpacking now. They bought a house that my grandfather and dad had built. Dad was surprised at how much the town has changed since we've been gone. There are so many new houses around. He was happy to see one for sale that was familiar to him."

"Oh, I'm glad to hear that. I know how important that was to him."

"He said he's planning to come see you as soon as we're settled."

A smile crossed David's lips. "I look forward to that. How are they, your parents?"

"They're okay now, I think. They've seemed like strangers to each other for a while, though. Dad's been busy working, and Mom's been busy with Grandma. I think she really has needed a break."

David felt a pain in his heart. He always thought of Scott and Clara as a great couple, a couple whose love would keep them close no matter what they went through. David opened the barn door, reached around for the light switch, and let Marie in ahead of him.

She stood inside looking around. Slowly she walked down the aisle, looking in each stall. She stopped at one and reached her hand in to scratch the forelock of a horse. "I think this is the one I fed the last time I was here."

David walked up to stand beside her and looked in. "I can picture it like it was yesterday. You seemed very shy then. You were quite a bit shorter too," he said laughingly.

"I really was shy and short. A lot has changed, I guess."

"You grew up a lot in Pennsylvania. What did you like to do there? I bet you had a lot of friends. Won't it be sad to be without them?"

Marie turned to continue walking until she reached a stool where she sat. "I enjoyed the school. Friends, I didn't really bother with. I was busy after school helping Mom with the house and taking care of Grandma."

"Was that hard on you? Sounds like you had to be responsible at a young age." David sat on a bale of hay facing her. "What did you do for yourself, for fun, I mean?"

"I didn't mind helping Mom. We became really close. It was nice. I guess it never felt like I needed friends. I read a lot, though. I do really enjoy that."

"What was your dad doing for work? Was he building?"

"He was building and remodeling houses, same as he did here."

"Business must've been good, then, if he was busy like you said."

"Yeah, Mom mentioned once she thought he was staying busy to avoid my grandmother."

"What do you think? I don't picture something like that bothering him."

"It was difficult, I think. They needed time alone, to talk and feel like they were a couple, but I think Dad got tired of listening to stories about my grandmother." Marie chuckled. "They didn't fight, just seemed to stop talking."

"That's sad." David's impression of his friend was altered.

"I know. I think the move will put everything right," Marie said.

"I hope so," David responded as he stood and walked to the door, looking out. "Marie, come see this."

She rose and went to his side, and her breath caught. "Beautiful!" she exclaimed.

"I come here at this time on nice days just to see this," he shared.

As the sun set, it cast beautiful colors across the few clouds peppered about the sky. The inn, nestled in the shadow below, looked charming with its lights glowing through the windows. The old barn exterior looked fabulous, framing the multi-paned windows filling much of the first floor. The balconies above were draped with flowering vines that had grown up, offering scented privacy.

"This is beautiful, Mr. Towell!" Marie exclaimed.

"Oh, please call me David," he offered.

Marie looked to him and smiled. "My dad often talks about you. He says you're one of a kind. That you're someone who takes pride in what you create and also, that you care about the people who work for you. He says that's not common. I'm happy things have been going well for you. Dad says you deserve it."

"Thank you, Marie. I'm happy doing what I do. I think I'm ready for change, though."

Marie stepped out the barn door, and David followed closing it behind them. They could hear the music drifting up the hill, which got louder briefly when someone opened the French door.

"My goodness, I'm sorry. You came here to dance, and I've taken up your time. Let's go back."

They walked down the path, returning to the inn.

"David?" Marie asked timidly.

"Yes?"

"Do you like to dance? Would you like to dance, I mean?" she asked.

David felt uncomfortable. "I'm sorry, Marie, I don't know how. I've never wanted to."

He felt bad once the words left his lips. She had just returned to town and came here tonight to dance. She was showing a confidence that impressed him.

"It's fine," she said.

They reached the steps to the terrace.

"Thanks for bringing me to see the horses and for the conversation. It's been nice to see you again," Marie said. "I can't wait for Dad to come here."

"Tell him hi for me. Please let him know I'm looking forward to seeing him again."

"Okay, I will." Marie trotted up the steps and opened the door, releasing the music once more into the darkening night. She turned back in the doorway and shouted, "Thanks again!"

David waved his hand to her and watched as she closed the door behind her.

13

David hired Scott back as the head carpenter. They spent many days working through ideas for the inn with Chance at their feet, just like old times. They talked about the growth of Roxboro, the events that had taken place at the inn in the last seven years, and Scott's life in Pennsylvania. He had done well with his carpentry business while living there, and it had been a helpful escape from life at home.

"It was really difficult, David," Scott eventually shared one early winter afternoon when they were working on some repairs. "Her mother was crazy. I mean really crazy. You don't just tell someone that, though. You can't let people know. Do you know what would have happened to us? I hated to think about it. Clara kept her home all the time, and we could never have company. Outside of walks in the yard, she was with us all the time."

David put his tools down and leaned against the wall to listen, shaking his head in amazement.

Scott turned and sat down beside him. "It didn't start out too bad. She was odd at first, talking to herself once in a while, but eventually it sounded like she was really having conversations with people. We just couldn't see them. She would talk about things that could never have happened, and she would argue as if you were the crazy one for not believing her. It was weird. I couldn't stand to be home after a while. I know Clara worked hard and needed a break just as much as I did, but I couldn't cope."

"So you worked," David offered.

"Yup, I worked," Scott answered. "I felt guilty, though. I made excuses that I was meeting our needs, that my work was important. I know it sounds mean, but I was glad when her mother became so sick she had to stay in bed. At least then I could have some space at home without dealing with her. When she died, it was a blessing. Clara's been through a lot. She worked really hard, every day for seven years."

"She must've felt so alone," David mused aloud.

"I never thought of that. She had Marie. I know I felt alone," Scott admitted.

"Did you ever talk about it?"

"Not 'til we came back here. We just needed to get through it I guess. Now we're here, we made it, and we can live our lives again."

"That's sad, though," David responded.

"I suppose it is," Scott said. "Seven years was a long time to wish most days away, let me tell you. So, David, a lot happened since we've been apart. The inn has done well regardless of war and the Spanish flu."

"Yes, we've been fortunate. The flu was rough to get through," David recollected. "I closed the inn for a few months including during the holidays that year. My staff fared well enough, though a couple of them lost relatives. I paid them half salaries while we were closed. It was a tough time for many."

"Any big, exciting events happen here?" Scott asked.

"I don't know if you ever met Cam Morrision. He came with his wife on our opening day."

Scott smiled. "I remember him clearly. He was a big guy, seemed so jovial."

"That's him. I've joined him on occasion at the state house in Raleigh. After he became governor, we worked together to get through some pretty big changes for the highways."

"I was hearing about that. It was big news," Scott pointed out.

"All that was after his wife died. It was an unexpected loss for him. He came here after she passed to be quiet and regroup."

"Sounds like you've been a good friend to him."

"I don't know. I think he just needed to be by himself, out of the politics. He needed some peace for himself and to pray for direction. His wife was such a supportive woman. I didn't know how he was going to do without her."

"He must've found his direction. He's doing pretty well now, right?"

"He is," David answered. "Things are going very well for him."

The men talked deep into the night, enjoying each other's company after a long time apart.

———✳︎———

The inn bustled throughout the holidays. The annual Thanksgiving feast was filled to capacity. Their Christmas pageant drew crowds from all over the Northeast, and the New Year's Eve bash had become the desire of dignitaries from all over the country.

When the chill of January produced a record snowfall, David hosted a sledding party behind the inn for the locals. A bonfire was lit, and hot chocolate was simmering in wait.

The amount of people that came was indicative of the support the community gave the Foxglove Inn. The sight of nearly a hundred local people dressed for snow and playing in the back yard made David feel proud. Chance didn't seem interested in the activities, though, and settled down to rest in the library.

"Are you sledding too?"

David turned to see Scott coming through the door bundled up in warm winter clothes followed by Clara and Marie.

"I wasn't planning on it," David answered.

Clara came and slid her arm through his. "Now, David, you can't be the host and not join the party. That would just seem impolite, don't you think?"

Scott laughed at the pressure his wife was putting on David.

Marie chuckled too and slid her hand through his other arm. "I think it is terribly impolite," she said.

He looked from side to side at the two women. "I really don't think I'm up for sliding, ladies."

"But, David," Marie continued, "I don't think I can if you don't."

"It sounds like you don't have many options, David, because my little girl really had her heart set on sliding tonight," Scott said with a grin.

"You know, I was thinking of the children in town when I sent out the word, not the old people."

"Huh," Clara said, dropping her hand from his arm. "Speak for yourself. Come, Marie, I won't take such insults." Clara reached her hand out in dramatic fashion for her daughter. The pair stormed out the back door, leaving the men behind laughing.

"Looks like you hurt the ladies' feelings, David," Scott pointed out.

"Looks like I'd better get my coat and gloves on," David answered.

He joined his guests and community members and even encouraged some of the staff to climb the hill and enjoy the snow. The moon rose, offering even more to the cheerful atmosphere. The bonfire was surrounded by many who rotated on occasion, keeping each side of them a little warmer. There were groups of kids laughing, adults sitting on the steps watching, and even some who had broken out into song.

David watched the crowd but often turned to look at the inn. Times were always changing, prompting him to think of new things to offer—events, bands, activities, upgrades to the build-ing, changes to the gardens. He had added a drama troupe in the fall to the list of regular entertainment, and that had been well received.

Scott came up beside him and handed him a mug of hot chocolate. Together they brainstormed, sipping their drinks. They decided it was time to add bathrooms. David was determined to keep the inn current, always evolving and always exciting for each guest, whether they were new or had been there many times before.

The girls eventually came off the hill, laughing and rosy cheeked. They stopped to see the men briefly before wandering off to warm at the fire with mugs of hot chocolate. David watched them while he and Scott continued their conversation. They were a close family, full of love and obviously strong enough to survive the most difficult of times. He remembered his view of them faltering when he heard of their emotional distance in Pennsylvania. He smiled now as he proudly realized he should not have underestimated the power of the unconditional love they obviously had for each other.

CHAPTER

14

Marie could hardly believe her eyes when she entered the Foxglove Inn. Her dad had asked her to meet him there once she was done doing her homework at the Roxboro Public Library. It was just after six o'clock, and they were going to have dinner there for her seventeenth birthday. She was looking forward to it.

She closed the door behind her but couldn't stop looking around at all the red roses and yellow daffodils. There was a large banner hanging below the upstairs landing in the great room that read, "Happy Birthday, Marie." Standing beneath the sign were her parents and David, all smiling. Other guests were milling around, looking at them curiously.

A waiter came forward. "Miss Tudor, could you come this way, please? Your table is ready."

She looked quizzically at the three watching her. David nodded to her, encouraging her to follow. She stepped forward, and the waiter led her through the dining room door. There was a table set for four adorned with a bouquet of roses and daffodils. On another table there was a large cake and an assortment of wrapped gifts. She walked up to the cake and saw the beautiful flowers made out of frosting, which tempted her to reach down and swipe a small amount. As she put her finger in her mouth, the door opened behind her.

"Hey, caught you!"

Marie turned to see David. She laughed before noticing the other diners watching them. "This is too much, David."

"Are you kidding? It's your seventeenth birthday. It is a big deal, and so, my dear, this certainly is not too much."

She smiled at him as she licked the remainder of the frosting off her finger. "Mmm, this is really good. Did Jonathan do this?"

"Actually, Sheila did. She's been working hard this afternoon."

Marie looked around. "Is she still here?"

"No, she left at five."

"I wish I could thank her. Will you be sure to tell her I loved it?"

"Of course, but she'll be in tomorrow. Come tell her yourself."

The door opened, and Marie's parents joined them.

"Well, what do you think, honey?" Clara asked as she settled her arm around her daughter's waist.

"This is wonderful, thank you. What a surprise! And all the flowers, they're beautiful."

Scott took Clara's hand and led his wife to the table. "Those were David's idea."

Marie looked at David, who was still standing beside her. "Yellow's my favorite color."

David led her to the table where he held her seat. "Somehow I knew that. The red was my idea, it suggests youthful beauty. The two colors do look great together, don't they?"

Marie sat and looked up at him. "They do. You put a lot of thought into them. Thank you."

Scott cleared his throat. "Enough with the thoughtful stuff, let's eat. I'm starving."

They enjoyed a meal of roast chicken, mashed potatoes, and sweet peas. When they had finished, David handed the first of the presents to Marie.

She looked at her parents, who had nestled closer to each other, holding hands. *That has been the best gift,* she thought. *Their happiness is priceless.*

She opened her first present. It was a book from her parents by Booth Tarkington, *Gentle Julia*.

"Thank you, Mom and Dad," Marie said as she rose to plant a kiss on each of their cheeks.

The next gift she opened from her parents contained matching gloves, hat, and parasol, all made of white lace. After that she unwrapped a beautiful yellow dress. David handed her one from him; it was a bracelet. She rose and planted a kiss on his cheek as well. The final gift was also from him, a framed painting of a horse.

"Thank you. What a wonderful picture," she said as she turned it to show her parents.

David rose from the table and asked her to follow him. "Put your coat back on. It's chilly out," he said.

Her parents smiled when she looked at them, making her more curious. David led her out the French doors and onto the terrace.

"Let's go for a walk, Marie."

Chance slipped through the door and joined them.

"But what about my parents? Isn't it rude leaving them behind?" she said playfully as she stretched down to pat the dog's head. It appeared they were in on the secret by the looks on their faces.

"Not rude at all. Besides, they're busy getting ready."

"Ready? Ready for what, David? What's going on?" she asked.

"You'll see shortly, but in the meantime I wanted you to meet the horse in the picture."

He took her by the hand and began running slowly as she laughed. She enjoyed being back in Roxboro. It felt like home, and she was very much enjoying her time spent at the inn. She felt as though she and David, even though he was thirteen years older, had the best friendship. They both seemed to be less than social in general but enjoyed each other's company. She wondered if he would let her work for him once school finished in June.

They went to the corral where there was a new horse trotting around acting nervous.

"He's magnificent, David, just like in the painting. I'll cherish it. Is he yours, or is someone boarding him here?"

Marie reached out to the pure-white Arabian. He stopped moving around and stepped forward cautiously until he was able to sniff at her outstretched hand with his pink nose.

"Do you like him?" David asked.

"Oh, I do. Look at him. How could I not? He's simply beautiful."

"Good, I'm glad," David said as he turned toward her. "I got him for you."

Marie looked abruptly to David's face. Her quick movement startled the horse, who stepped away, tossing his head. "You're kidding, right? No, David. This can't be." She was caught between feeling terrible at such an expensive gift, absolutely horrible, and a feeling akin to euphoria. Tears came to her eyes. "David, I can't accept this."

"Well, I certainly hope you can, because he's here to stay, and I was really hoping to have a riding partner. Storm, that two-year-old that was born here, needs some training, and I thought we could get them out together."

Marie stared long and hard at the horse once more then turned her wet eyes back to David. The tears overflowed and spilled down her cheeks just then as she threw her arms around his neck. She held tight and cried as David patted her back, laughing.

"Marie. Marie. Hey, don't cry," he said.

"Don't laugh at me," she said from the crook of his neck.

"What, did I make you upset? I didn't mean to make you upset. Please."

After a moment Marie released her hold and sank back to the ground, looking once more to the corral. The horse had trotted away and was joining the others. "I don't know what to say."

"Just say you'll ride with me," he suggested.

She nodded her head, slowly at first then more sincerely. "I will."

"Good. I have one more request from you for this evening.'"

Marie looked at David. "What else could there possibly be?"

"Well, the band is setting up now, and people are arriving. I heard cars pulling up the drive since we've been out here."

"Why? What's going on?"

"There's a sweet young girl turning seventeen today, and I thought she might enjoy a swinging, good dance, even though it's Monday."

Marie jumped with excitement, her heart racing. "Really? A dance tonight, for me?"

"I remember how excited you were the night you first came back to Roxboro, so I talked with your parents about bringing in a jazz band tonight. Who would've thought your mother would be as excited as I only hoped you'd be."

"She was? Of course she was! She loves to dance too! We dance to the radio all the time. Oh, David, this is going to be so much fun." A squeal of excitement escaped her lips.

"Wait, what about my request?" he asked.

"I forgot. I'm sorry, David. What is it?" She could hardly contain her excitement and wasn't even paying attention to his nervousness.

"Will you dance with me?"

Marie was quickly brought back to her senses, and she looked at him with concern on her face.

David laughed. "Don't look so worried."

"I'm not worried. I just feel bad. I know you don't dance. I understand. You don't have to dance with me."

"Don't have to? I know I don't have to. I want to. Only one, though, and it'll have to be a slow one. The fancy dancing people do today is just too confusing for me."

Marie reached out and held his arm, covering her mouth with her other hand to hide her chuckle. "A slow dance would be fine. You don't have to, though."

"It isn't out of obligation, Marie. I really want to as a birthday present for you."

"Oh, David." She looked down at her outfit, realizing she was not dressed for a dance, when it struck her that she had opened the most appropriate dress for such an occasion. "Is that why…?"

David nodded, and Marie rose up to kiss his cheek before running back to the inn to get ready.

CHAPTER

15

While the girls were getting ready for their big night of dancing and the band was setting up, the men sat at one of the tables in the great room.

"I told Marie I'd dance with her tonight," David confessed.

Scott laughed. "Now whatever possessed you to do that?"

"It's her birthday, and she likes to dance. Besides, I let her down when you guys first came back to North Carolina. I wouldn't dance with her when she asked."

"You know, David, I'm beginning to think you're sweet on her," Scott said.

David glanced at his friend, who was laughing. "She's a good kid," he responded defensively.

"She's a good woman," Scott pointed out.

David became quiet. A good woman. She did seem mature, but a woman? Slowly, and deep in thought now, David got up and wandered out of the great room, and though the music was starting up and was loud, it seemed faint to him. He saw Marie dancing with her mother. She was laughing, and yes, she looked beautiful in her yellow gown. She caught sight of him and waved. David nodded in acknowledgement.

How funny it was that a simple comment could change the outlook of something. Would it not be inappropriate for him to care for his best friend's daughter? Would it not seem inappropriate that he was so much older than she? David looked at Scott happily clapping while watching his wife dance with their daughter. David felt awkward and uncomfortable at this moment and, skirting the group in the room, wandered out to the terrace and the chill of the early night air. He leaned against the railing and inhaled deeply.

With a sigh he spoke. "Lord, I'm confused right now. I don't know what to think or what I'm feeling. I care for Marie, of course I do. She's the daughter of my good friend, and she's my close friend. Do I love her? Is that what I feel? Would it be wrong to love her? Please help me understand."

The French door opened, interrupting David's prayer. He opened his eyes and casually looked over his shoulder to find Marie, shrugging her jacket on over her new dress. His heart jumped unsure if this was God's answer.

"David, is something wrong?" Her voice was quiet.

He turned to face her. "No, just trying to build my courage for our dance." He smiled, hopefully putting her at ease.

"I told you that you don't have to. I don't want you to feel uncomfortable. I'm fine with us not dancing."

"I like that about you, Marie. You do care what others feel. Thank you. However, this time I have a gift to give you, and I do believe the music is slow right now."

Marie cocked her head to hear the change the tempo had taken. David put his arms out for her. She laughed, and this time her laughter tugged differently at his heart. She stepped into his arms, and they began to waltz slowly with the beat of the music.

He could smell her hair, and the touch of her arm on his shoulder made him swallow hard. He held her hand in his; it was soft and small, and it made him feel as though he should protect her always. He looked down at her. She was smiling up at him. He returned the cheer with a smile of his own.

"So, when are we going to start riding?" she asked.

"Would Saturday be too soon?" he suggested.

"Not for me."

David felt warmth fill his heart as he looked at her sparkling eyes. "Not for me either. Have you enjoyed your birthday?"

"This has been the best birthday ever."

"Good, that's what we wanted for you."

They were waltzing in the light of a crescent moon and chatting like old friends when the door opened, and Scott stepped onto the terrace, pulling Clara by the hand. "Here, let's dance here."

"Why can't we dance on the dance floor, Scott?" Clara asked. "Are you afraid of dancing in front of people?"

David chuckled, drawing their attention.

Scott pointed at them. "There, see. David and Marie are here. They're people. Besides, I thought it'd be romantic under the stars."

"Yeah, right, and it's cold out here," Clara said, rolling her eyes at her husband before turning her attention to the others. "Hi, Marie and David. Do you mind if we join you?" Clara lowered her voice to a loud whisper and leaned toward her daughter. "I think your father's afraid to dance in public."

Marie's chuckle turned into a full laugh when her father grabbed her mother by the wrist and pulled her clumsily into his arms. "Let me hold you and keep you warm," Scott said, wrapping his arms around his wife.

The two pairs danced in silence, listening to the music.

When the song finished, the tempo picked up, but the dancers continued their waltzing as one by one Scott, Clara, and David wished Marie a very happy birthday.

———∿∾◦◌⟨◦⟩◦∾∿———

It was Saturday, and Marie had the day free to get to know her horse. David met her at the corral with bagged lunches for their travels.

"First and most importantly, you need to have a name for your horse," David suggested.

"What was his name before?"

"I don't believe he had one."

"He must've had one. I wouldn't want to confuse him now," Marie said with concern in her voice.

"Really, I never heard of one if he had. What do you think of when you see him?"

Marie crossed her arms and looked at him. Then she rubbed her chin and walked a bit, pacing back and forth slowly.

"Well?" David asked impatiently.

"This is a really important decision. Don't rush me." She continued looking as though deep in thought.

David leaned against the fence and smiled at her. She made him laugh. She had such a pure spirit. She was sweet and caring, beautiful and funny. He felt happy just being with her.

"Okay, I think I've got it," she said. "How about Duplin?"

"Duplin, what kind of name is that?" David stood straight again.

"It was a name in a book I just read."

"Really, Duplin?" David asked again as he walked to stand beside her. He looked at the horse. "I don't know about that. I don't see it."

"The character in the book was a regal man who stood up for what was good." Pointing toward the horse, Marie continued her argument. "Look at him. He's pure white. That represents goodness, and his Arabian features make him look regal."

"Regal?" Nodding in agreement, David added, "I guess he does look like he could be from royalty." He handed her one of the leads he had brought. "Okay, you get Duplin, while I get Storm, and we'll see about getting them saddled up."

"Has he been trained? I didn't ask anything about him Monday night." Marie stopped short. "Boy, I'm sorry. How stupid of me. I was so excited that I didn't pay any more attention to this gift."

David laughed. "No need to be sorry. It was understandable. It was a busy night." She had no idea how difficult a night it really had been for him emotionally.

CHAPTER

16

"David, I've been looking for you. It's Saturday. Aren't we going riding?" Marie stood outside David's office door, waiting to see if he would answer her knock. She had looked everywhere else and was worried now. They had been riding every Saturday since her birthday, and she looked forward to this special time with him. She was confused by her feelings, if truth be told. He was nearly as old as her parents, and was her father's closest friend, but she felt like he was her best friend. He was handsome too and very kind to her.

"Trisha, have you seen David? I'd expected to meet him at the barn."

"No," Trisha answered. "I'm sorry, Marie, I haven't seen him since yesterday."

Marie walked out the door and looked around the front of the inn before returning to Duplin at the corral. She rubbed his head absentmindedly, unsure if she should saddle him. She had put his halter and reigns on before looking for David. Now she was hoping he was okay when a distant bark caused her to look up.

Chance was running full speed over the hill toward the inn. She whistled sharply to catch his attention, stopping his run dead. He looked in her direction and then resumed his run toward her. Her heart began beating fast; something was wrong.

"Chance! What's wrong, boy?" Marie hollered.

He ran to her side and barked at her, which caused Duplin to pull away in alarm.

She reached down to try to calm him. "Okay, boy, okay."

He dodged her hand and ran back the way he came then stopped and barked again.

"Okay, now I know something's wrong." She went to Duplin, quickly led him out of the corral, climbed the fence, and jumped on his bare back. Digging her heels into his sides, she followed Chance, who was now racing back up the hill.

Marie's heart was pounding while she thought the worst. What was she going to find? Was David badly hurt or dead even? She couldn't imagine not spending time with him ever again. The very thought made her dig her heels in again, causing Duplin to gallop a little faster. It was hard racing along bareback. She held tightly to his mane and huddled close to his neck as he crested the hill. She glanced about, looking for the dog. Down the hill to the left along the treeline, she saw Chance standing at the entrance to the trail used to take guests on horseback rides. She turned Duplin in Chance's direction just as he disappeared down the trail.

Slowing down considerably, she guided Duplin onto the trail, where she had to be careful of the trees and rocks around them. The trail rides provided by the Foxglove Inn were slow journeys meant for relaxation. The trails offered all varieties of experiences with sections leading through a stream, some woodsy hills, and some breaks into open fields. The horses were all led in single file since the trail, in most places, was narrow.

Marie was anxiously looking about and straining for any sign of either Chance or David.

"David! David!" Her voice wavered with fear now.

Storm had still been at the stable; she was sure she had checked that. How far into the woods could he have gone? Just then she heard Chance's bark. It seemed close now. She peered around.

"David, where are you?" Marie pled loudly. She felt the fear overwhelm her, giving her a lump in her throat and causing her eyes to tear. "David!"

She saw Chance coming back to the trail through the woods. Quickly, she slid off Duplin, wrapped the reins around a tree branch, and ran into the woods to follow, but he ran off again. The brush was thick in spots, and she was worried she might get hurt herself as she scrambled over large boulders. She could not imagine, at this point, what David was doing out here.

"Marie, I'm here."

She stopped to peruse the area from which she heard his faint voice. "David. I can't see you." Marie climbed around a large boulder and walked around a shrub when she finally saw Chance's tail.

"I'm here, on the ground." David's voice was closer now.

Marie got all the way around the shrub and saw David sitting on the ground with Chance at his side. His face looked pale, and he was holding his leg, what she could see of it. She dropped to his side.

"Are you okay?"

He smiled weakly. "Sorry I missed our date."

She looked him over in order to find the reason for his situation and was horrified to see one of his legs pinned under a boulder. "Oh my goodness, David, I'd say it's a good thing we had a date. Otherwise, you might not have been found. What happened?"

"Look up there." David pointed a finger toward an outcropping of rocks that jutted out a couple hundred feet above them.

Marie looked but was unsure of what he was pointing at. "Is there something up there?"

"I can see those rocks from the hill in the pasture, and I've wanted to check them out for some time."

She turned her attention back to David's leg. "Did you go up there?"

"I tried, but some of the rocks gave way, and I slid down with them. That's how my leg got caught. I can't seem to free it." David smiled and patted the boulder as if it was a pet.

"Are you hurt? Do you think your leg's broken? You look pale."

"I feel bumped up a bit. My back's sore," David answered.

"What about your leg?" Marie asked.

"I have a feeling I'm just stuck. It doesn't hurt when I wiggle my toes."

"Okay, let me try to figure this out." Marie walked around carefully on the loose stones, trying not to fall. She got down on her knees and looked closely at his trapped leg. "I'm afraid I'm going to crush your leg if I move any of them."

"I hope not," David said with a pained grin on his face, "because I don't think you're strong enough to carry me if I can't walk."

Marie took a deep breath. The biggest fear she had was finding him dead. Those thoughts had devastated her, and now she realized how happy she was that she found him like this.

"Well"—she looked up at him—"if you don't think you're hurt, and you certainly don't look as pale as when I first saw you, then I suppose this is just the opportunity I needed to ask for a favor."

David's eyes grew wide with surprise then softened as his lips curled into a smile. "Really? Taking advantage of an injured man? That doesn't sound like you, Marie."

"Oh no, sir. I'm taking advantage of a trapped man. I would never take advantage of someone who's injured. That would be mean." Marie chuckled as she sat back on a larger stone and began to think intently. "Let's see. Hmm, I think I'd like one dance with you next Friday night."

"Wait a minute, that's not fair."

"Not fair? Well, I think I should just go home." Marie stood up and turned as if to go. "I think Mother would love help cleaning today."

"A dance, you say?" His answer was quick and loud.

She turned back toward him. "That's what I said, but since you argued, I think I'll make it one every Friday night."

In this game Marie had begun, she felt her heart racing with excitement. She looked down at his expression and felt like a giddy schoolgirl with a crush. A blush came over her cheeks.

He nodded his head slowly in response. "Okay, every Friday night I'll dance with you. Just one though, right? A slow one."

Marie clapped her hands and lifted her head, proudly the winner. "Okay, it can be slow." That was her goal, after all. She wanted him to hold her. There was something comforting about that birthday dance they shared.

"Now, can you help me get out of here?" he asked.

CHAPTER

17

The music was loud, the air was brisk for an April night, the stars sparkled, and they danced alone on the terrace. David was limping, and after spending nearly a week out of commission, he was ready to make good on his promise.

He held her close, breathing in her scent as they swayed to the music. While trapped in the woods, he prayed about his feelings for this beauty he now held in his arms, and when she appeared, his heart was elated. His prayers were not desperate, they were requests for direction.

That day, as he watched her carefully consider how to best free him and how best to care for him as they struggled back to the trail, he knew in confidence the time was upon them.

He watched Marie as she was looking up at the stars. She was radiant. "You never asked me why I was in the woods to begin with on Saturday."

She lowered her eyes to look at him. "I thought you said you were checking out the rocks you could see from the pasture."

"I was, but there was a reason," he stated. He faltered subtly in his dance steps.

Marie stopped moving. "David, let's sit and talk. You're still sore," she offered.

David pulled her form straight and continued their dancing. "I was blackmailed into this dance, and I intend to follow through."

"Okay." She seemed to appear concerned now and kept an eye to his leg. "Do share why you were in the woods."

"It was for you."

"For me, you mean it's my fault you were injured? You're blaming me?" she asked.

David laughed at her look of shock. "Yes, as a matter of fact, it was."

"Please explain."

"Well, you're finishing school in a few weeks, and I wanted to find a special place to share with you, a place that we could picnic in celebration of your graduation. That spot with the rocks, I think, would look over the land. That would be a nice place to take you."

As the slow song came to an end, David took Marie's hand and led her down the stairs to the bench in the yard. "I'm sorry, I have to sit," he said.

"I'm sorry," she answered. "You shouldn't be dancing."

"I would've been left out there for the wild animals to get if I hadn't agreed to this." David's attempt at jest brought a tinge of sadness to Marie's face. "I'm sorry, honey. I was only teasing. I wanted to dance with you tonight. Your blackmail simply was the excuse."

The smile came back to her face.

He called her honey. It had rolled off his tongue so easy. He was falling deeply in love with her and wanted to take care of her, to bring her joy always. His heart fluttered, which brought a smile to his lips.

"I think it'd be nice to clear a trail up to the top of those rocks."

"What a great idea!" Marie exclaimed. "It'd be a fantastic spot for guests to have a picnic lunch during trail rides! Would you like me to help?"

She wasn't listening to his plan.

David continued, "My goal was to celebrate your graduation in June. Marie, I was thinking of us. We can open it up for the public after, if that's what you want."

Marie grabbed David's hands in hers. "That'd be so much fun! Would you really like my help?"

David looked at their hands, his surrounded by hers. "Of course I want your help. Tell you what, tomorrow and each Saturday until we're done, which will hopefully be in time for graduation, we'll work instead of ride."

———wwoooerooooweoowww———

They started planning the route then worked hard using the power of the horses to pull limbs out of the way. They cleared a spot just off the main trail for the trail horses to stay while guests walked the remaining route to the top of the outcropping.

The view was beautiful, just as David had suspected. There was a wonderful area, which didn't need much attention to make it perfect at the top. It proved spacious enough to allow a group of a dozen or more people to gather, spread out a blanket if they wanted, and enjoy the view overlooking two directions, one of which was the inn.

In the four weekends working up to Marie's graduation, they had all the work David said he wanted done. Now they sat on the overlook together, enjoying it.

"Next Saturday's the day, Marie. You mentioned once that you wanted to work for me at the inn when you graduate. Is that still something you'd like to do?"

"I was hoping to talk to my parents about it. If they're agreeable, is it something you feel I could do?" she asked.

"Well, you're a hard worker. I think you'd be great for business. You know everything about the inn. What do you think you'd like to do here?"

"I like working with the horses the most. Could I work in the barn? I could take guests on the trail rides, and I could tell them about all this work we did while we picnic!"

David had ideas for her future as well and hoped she would be accepting of them. They ate a late afternoon snack of apples he had taken from the kitchen. He watched her as she munched away, looking deep in thought.

"David, can I ask you a personal question?"

"Of course," he answered.

"You seem like a wonderful man. How is it that you've never married?"

Her question caught him off guard, and he choked on the apple as he caught his breath. "What made you think of that?"

"How could I not? My parents have been married for a long time, and it made me think you should've married some time ago."

"Is this something you've really wondered?" he asked her.

"I have," she answered.

"Well, I guess I hadn't married for a few reasons."

"Really?" David could see her glance at him from the corner of her eyes and then look away again.

"First of all, my parents were very unhappy, they could not have loved each other. They argued all the time, which made it very uncomfortable for me. I never wanted to marry if it meant unhappiness for the rest of my life or someone else's. I couldn't imagine living like that."

Marie nodded.

"And secondly, I've been busy. I haven't had the time to devote to someone, and I don't think that would be fair to a wife waiting at home, do you?" He looked curiously at Marie and watched as she slowly turned her attention to him.

"I suppose not," she answered.

David watched Marie's distant look before he spoke. "I think our work is done here. I've something special for you. I'll show you next Sunday during our celebration picnic, okay?"

Marie stood up. "Sure, that'd be great."

He could detect sadness in her tone. "Come on. Let's go." He stood and let her lead the way back down the trail.

CHAPTER

18

Marie's graduation ceremony ended at eleven thirty on the morning of Saturday, June 13, 1925. Thirty students from her class graduated with her, most of which she did not know well. Since the Foxglove Inn had opened, many more families had moved to the area. The school had a lot to do to keep up with the growth. She was surprised at the differences when she had returned in the fall after seven years away.

Her parents had taken her shopping for a new dress for the occasion, and she simply glowed wearing it.

"Mom, that was exciting!" Marie exclaimed, holding up her diploma.

"I know, honey. I'm so proud of you." Clara held her daughter's arms and looked her over.

As she smiled, Marie sensed something different in her mother's demeanor. "Mom, are you okay?"

"Of course, I'm just happy." Clara pulled her daughter to her and held her tight. "You're so grown up, and I think you've become such a wonderful woman, Marie."

"Thanks, Mom."

The pair separated as Clara brushed the tears from her eyes. "What do you say we head home to celebrate?"

"That sounds great!" Marie took Clara's hand, and the pair walked to Scott and David, who were waiting by their cars. "Thanks for coming, David," Marie said.

"Wouldn't have missed it for the world, Marie," David answered.

"You're joining us for lunch, David?" Clara asked. "I was expecting you to come."

"I'll be there shortly. I need to get something for the graduate."

David winked at Clara as he turned to get in his car, causing Marie to question her mother. "Hey, what's going on here?"

"Oh, it's nothing, darling." Clara smiled, draped her arm around her daughter's shoulders, and led her to their car. "Soon enough," Clara said quietly with a smile.

The Tudor family went home to enjoy a celebratory lunch of cucumber sandwiches, shrimp cocktail, and lemonade followed by a graduation cake Clara had made.

"That was delicious, Mom!" Marie exclaimed after finishing her piece. "Thank you for doing this." Marie motioned to the streamers decorating their home. It looked festive and made her feel very special.

Clara chuckled. "You're welcome. It was fun getting ready, though I didn't exactly have a lot of time. I was able to make the cake while you were at the inn last night, that was a help, but the streamers took a long time to put up. I waited for you and your father to leave for the school, but it wasn't enough time. He had to help me finish when he came back to get me. We were almost late to see our only daughter graduate."

Marie laughed. "Well, it was worth it. It looks great, Mom."

Scott threw open the front door, causing Marie to jump as he rushed in. "Oh my goodness, Dad! You scared me!"

"David's here!" he yelled excitedly, and Clara rose from the table.

Marie looked at her. "Mom, what? What's wrong? We were expecting him. Why are you surprised?"

"No, nothing's wrong, Marie," Clara responded with a grin on her face.

Scott grabbed Marie's hand and pulled her to the door with him. "Come on! He's here!"

"I know. He said he was coming. What's going on?" She turned to question her mother, who joined her husband and pushed Marie through the doorway.

The three stepped out onto the porch, and Marie looked around quizzically. "Where? I don't see him."

"There," Clara said, pointing excitedly.

Marie followed her mother's direction. "I don't see…" Her words trailed off as she saw David pulling his head out of a car she did not recognize, holding a very large bow, which he placed on top. Marie stood on the porch, feeling confused.

"Hi Marie, sorry I'm late!" David yelled up to her from the road, sounding rather casual. "I got you a little something."

"What do you mean?" Marie asked.

"Honey, go down there," Clara whispered as she pushed at her daughter's back.

"What? Okay, I'm going."

Marie hesitantly walked down the stairs, holding on to the railing as she looked back at her parents. Her father's arm was around her mother's shoulders, and though she was smiling, it looked like her mother was tearing up.

"What's going on?"

"I thought it was time you learned to drive, Marie, and since I couldn't think of a graduation present fitting enough, I asked your parents if they wouldn't mind if I got you a car." At those final words, David stepped back, waving his arm toward the light yellow Mercedes-Benz before her.

As if it might bite her, Marie stepped cautiously toward the new car parked at the curb in front of her house. She mulled his words over, but they weren't really registering. *I got you a car. I got you a car.* This was her present? She stopped by David's side when the truth of the situation hit. She looked it all over slowly; then her mouth dropped wide open.

"Oh my goodness, David, I can't accept a car! I can't accept this gift from you." She began shaking her head slowly.

"That's too bad, because I special ordered it, and I can't take it back now." David smiled and watched as her confusion turned to amazement, and then in a heartbeat, she was wrapped around his neck with tears rolling down her cheeks.

"David, thank you!" She clung tightly but briefly then returned to her own feet. "When will you teach me?"

"How about after I finish eating lunch?" David suggested.

"Oh!" Marie clasped her hands together in pure delight. "Oh, I can't wait!"

Clara and Scott came to stand beside them.

"David, that's a beautiful gesture," Clara said. "Thank you so much."

"Yes, thank you," Scott chimed in.

"No, don't thank me. I'm thankful you're supporting my plans." With a wink to Clara, he continued, "Now, I know I'm late, but I'm famished. Is there any food left?"

"Absolutely, come on in," Clara offered, taking David by the arm and leading him up the stairs, leaving Marie and Scott behind with her new gift.

"He's a fabulous guy, Marie," her father offered.

"Fabulous? I know, but this is too much, Dad." Marie had her arms crossed and kept looking the car over as she wiped at the wetness on her cheeks.

"I don't know, honey. I think David really cares about you. He wants to make sure you have everything you need."

His words hit her sharply then pleasantly sank in, bringing a smile to her lips. Perhaps, oh, just perhaps he did have an attraction for her. She had been thinking about him often since he got hurt. She realized she had deeper feelings for him than just friendship and was now really hoping he might, in some way, feel the same. She surely wasn't about to embarrass herself by letting him know she was in love with him.

The excitement within caused Marie to squeal with joy. "Oh, Daddy. I can't believe this! Let's get in, shall we?"

Marie's father stood grinning as he watched his daughter. He cleared his throat, causing her to look up at him as she reached for the door handle.

"Don't you think you should be getting in the driver's seat?"

Marie giggled and blushed before rushing around the car to open the driver's side door. She climbed in and sank deeply into the seat, only barely noticing her father as he slid into the passenger seat beside her. She caressed each and every knob, surface, and gadget.

"Marie, this car is just right for you."

A smile spread across her lips as she held the steering wheel tightly. "Do you really think so, Daddy?"

"I do," her father answered. He watched her as she imagined she was driving on the interstate. "I do," he repeated.

CHAPTER

19

David spent the afternoon of graduation day teaching Marie to drive. He had laughed so hard due to her unpredictable maneuvers that he claimed his stomach hurt. She feigned hurt feelings but enjoyed the laughter and was thrilled she could drive now, a little anyway. When she pulled up to the curb in front of her house, she invited him to join them for dinner. David politely declined the offer and reminded her they had special plans in the morning. Marie relinquished her seat to him as she was not yet licensed, and he drove away.

Marie enjoyed a wonderful night with her parents. After dinner, they sat in the yard star gazing and chatting. The night seemed to fly by, but when it was time for bed, Marie could hardly sleep. She and David had special plans, and morning wasn't coming soon enough.

She awoke multiple times during the night, this time the sun was rising, and Marie decided she could not wait any longer to get out of bed. Creeping quietly to the kitchen, where she thought she would sit with a cup of tea while waiting for the day to move on, she was surprised to find her mother already there.

"Mom, you're up early," Marie whispered so as not to wake her father.

"Good morning, honey," Clara answered quietly. "I couldn't sleep. Too much excitement, I guess." She rose from her seat and went to the stove. "Can I get you a cup of tea?"

"Yes, please," Marie answered.

Marie pulled her chair out quietly and sat down, watching her mother's back. After a few moments, Clara turned back toward the table with a cup of tea in her hands for Marie.

"You're up early too. Has the excitement of yesterday got you sleepless?"

"I suppose it should have, but I'm excited for today."

Clara nodded.

"I can't wait for the guests to go to the overlook and see how beautiful it is," Marie said. "Mom, did David talk to you about me working for him?"

Clara smiled at this question but shook her head. "No. He didn't mention anything about that. Why? Have you been talking about working for him?"

"I asked him if I could after graduating. You and Dad shouldn't keep taking care of me. I really need to start taking care of myself now."

Clara nodded slowly while gazing at her daughter. "I suppose you're right about that."

"Well, that's why I'm excited about opening the overlook to the public. I want to work in the barn, and I want to be the one to take the guests on trail rides so I can share it with them."

Marie was getting so excited that her mother put a finger to her mouth to quiet her.

Her voice returned to a whisper as she continued, "I'm sorry. See, I'm excited."

"I know, honey. I'm glad you feel this way. I hope you have a great day. It's hard to believe you're a graduate ready to step out on your own. I'm realizing how much you're a part of my life as I think of you moving on."

"Mom, it's a job, and with the money I'll make, I'll take care of myself more, so you'll have more for the two of you. It's not like I'm moving out or anything, not yet at least. It won't feel any different than if I were in school, really."

Clara nodded. "I know, dear. I love you and hope your future's all you want it to be. I'm excited for you."

They sat quietly as they finished their tea, each deep in thought.

Marie skipped up the path to the stables, feeling elated. The excitement of life itself had her bubbling with joy. With her school years behind her, the prospects of work before her, and the freedom of a car, she felt grown up. Her parents would have more of their lives to themselves now, and that made Marie happy. All of these things were spilling around in her head as she opened the barn door, a bit earlier than planned, and slipped in to see Duplin.

"Hey, Marie, how was your night?" David's voice startled her.

"Oh, hi, David."

"I'm sorry, I didn't mean to surprise you," he said.

"I didn't expect you to be here. I'm early. I have to admit, I didn't sleep well, and since I got up early, I thought I'd come by and visit with Duplin while waiting for our trail time."

"You didn't sleep well? Is everything okay?" David had a look of concern on his face as he rose from the hay bale he was sitting on. He put the tack down that he was working on.

Marie laughed. "Everything's fine. I think I said that wrong." She walked up to David and put a hand on his arm as she laughed. "Don't worry."

He smiled as if relieved. "Have a seat if you'd like, Marie." She sat on a bale of hay across from him as he returned to his work. "Tell me what had you missing sleep."

"Nothing really. I've been excited for our picnic. I can't wait to open the overlook to the public."

"You know," David said as he looked at her, "my goal was to celebrate you up there."

"Oh, David, that's not necessary. I think it's great that you found that spot, and soon, once I'm working for you, I can bring the trail groups up there and share it with them." She looked at David, who had a smirk on his face. "What are you smiling at?"

"You're bringing the trail groups up there?"

"Well, I thought we'd talk more about it later, but as you know, I was hoping you'd hire me."

David chuckled and returned his attention to the leather in his hands.

"What are you laughing at? This is important to me. I'm a graduate, and I'm looking for gainful employment." Marie became quiet as she contemplated a future for her parents as a couple. "That's what kept me up. I'm excited, David. My parents deserve to focus on each other now, and my working will help. I need to start looking at my future too, you know."

Again, David chuckled.

"Why do you think this is funny? My plans are well thought out. They make sense, and they benefit more than just me. That's how you plan things. At least that's what I've learned by watching you."

"Really?" David asked. "You've been watching me?"

"You know what I mean." She looked searchingly at David, imploring him to find value in her mission. "David, don't laugh at me."

He stood and stepped to her side. "I'm sorry, honey. You're right, and I don't want you to think I'm laughing at you. It's just, I've been thinking about all the same things. It's kind of ironic."

Marie's heart fluttered at his familiarity. He called her honey, and it sounded so good. No, she could feel her attention straying from the topic at hand. She refocused and responded, "No kidding, have you really?" She looked up at him as he was nodding, and she rose to stand facing him. Butterflies were filling her

insides, and she was finding this foolishness within her distract-
ing. "You're not joking?"

"No, that's why I got you a car. I agree it's time you live a more
adult life. I wasn't really looking at it in respect to your parents'
freedom from you, but more, well, simply for you."

Desperately trying to refocus her attention to her future,
Marie continued questioning her friend, "So, you agree that I
should work for you?"

"Marie, are you ready to hit the trail?"

With that statement, Marie remembered how all of this
excitement began. "Oh, my, you're right. We'll talk about this
later, though, David."

He chuckled as he turned to Storm's stall with the halter and
reigns in his hand. "I'm sure we will."

CHAPTER

20

The sun was high by the time they hit the trail. The apple trees were laden with growing fruit, and the grass was tall in the pasture. The birds were singing, and a wild rabbit ran through the field ahead of them, which Chance would have loved had he joined them. The sight of it prompted David to share the story that began his journey in Roxboro, the story of the second chance for a rabbit and for this property. Marie listened with great intent to his words and was surprised when his story revealed a trust in God.

They rode side by side through the field at a slow pace, stopping on occasion as their conversation dictated. Of all the times they had spent together, this was by far the most enjoyable for Marie. She had always been impressed by David's personality, the peace he shared with everyone he talked to, and his giving nature. Now she understood, he was a man of deep faith. She had not heard him talk about his relationship with God before. She was in awe at the simplicity of it, at the matter-of-fact manner in which David believed that God was in control of his life.

"You can't just leave everything to chance and claim it's God, though. That just seems naïve," Marie commented.

Everything he was saying made sense. His simple belief made it convincing to her—prayer being a discussion, not a ritual, seeking guidance and then actually knowing you are getting it. He made it sound believable as he was talking about it, but it just seemed unrealistic.

"It's not just leaving things to chance, Marie. It's giving God control, trusting that He knows what's best. I can't make someone believe in God, and I don't intend to try..."

"I believe in God," Marie interrupted. "I just don't think you can live the way you're describing."

"There's a difference between believing in God and having a relationship with him," David added.

"See, that's what doesn't make sense. How can you have a relationship with something you can't even see?"

"That's a question only God can answer for you, my dear." David smiled.

"Okay, how can God answer that question?" she asked.

"Just ask him. Ask him if he's real and if you can have a relationship with him."

"Oh, I don't know about that. Besides, I'm sure God's too busy to have conversations with me." Marie kicked her heels into Duplin's sides, urging him into a gallop and avoiding the question of God's interest in her. She looked back and shouted, "I'll meet you at the overlook!"

David acted quickly, bringing Storm to a full gallop, closing the gap between them as they raced to the pull off.

———————

They both reached the spot they had cleared for the overlook at the same time. Marie dismounted first, laughing, and David watched her with warmth in his heart.

He had come up here early this morning, not sleeping well himself for the uncertain excitement that was welling up within him. Her laughter hung in the air and sounded sweet to his ears. He dismounted and wrapped the reins around one of the bars they had positioned on either side of the clearing. After rummaging around his saddlebag, he pulled out the pack holding their lunch. Marie joined him.

"This is exciting!" she exclaimed.

"I'm glad you feel that way, Marie." He heard the tone of nervousness in his own voice and smiled quickly to try to cover it.

"Don't you feel that way too? David, aren't you excited?"

"I am." Though his tone implied nonchalance, his insides were churning with untamed butterflies.

"You don't show it. You're always calm, though, aren't you?" Marie snaked her arm through his. "Are you ready?"

"Yes, dear, I am."

They walked together until the path narrowed; then David waited for Marie to step forward and go up to the overlook first. It was only a short hike up from their point of separation, and David watched Marie from behind, his heart racing.

When she rounded the final curve and stepped up the last few stones, he stopped. She disappeared out of sight, and David waited as he uttered a prayer, "Lord, I trust you're here with me as I step out on faith toward a future I've spent many years avoiding. A future that will honor you, Lord."

There was silence but for the sounds of chirping chickadees. Time seemed to stop as David waited for a reaction from Marie.

She popped her head around the boulder that she had last disappeared behind and looked at him. Slowly, she stepped out and stood before him. She was so beautiful.

"Well," he asked, "what do you think?"

She walked up to him before answering in a calm and quiet voice, "David. It's wonderful."

"I thought you might like it. I wanted it to be extra special."

"Come," she took David's hand and pulled him to follow her back around the boulder.

He looked around, trying to see it from her point of view. He had purchased a hundred red roses and twice as many yellow daffodils. The florist had informed him that fifty red roses indicated unconditional love. If that was true, then, he figured twice as many would cover both of them. It certainly made a statement.

"I brought a surprise for you, Marie."

"A surprise, like this isn't surprise enough?"

"It's a special day, after all. Stay right there." He stepped around a set of trees that were in bloom and smelled fragrant and returned carrying something heavy draped in cloth. David brought it to the edge of the large boulder they were standing on and gently placed it on a flat spot in the dirt, which he had prepared earlier.

"What's that?" Marie appeared excited once again.

"You've worked hard with me getting this site ready for today," David said. "I had a plan for this place. It was going to be for the two of us to celebrate you graduating into a new life. Mine was a selfish plan. Yours was a goal that will benefit others. I love that you look at things and think of others, not yourself."

"What do you mean? You mentioned creating this spot. Why not share it with your guests? Didn't you want that? I'm sorry." Marie held her hand to her lips, suddenly looking embarrassed. "Oh, David, I'm sorry."

"That's what I mean. Don't be sorry. Your idea's beautiful, and I fully support it." There was so much more on his lips at that moment, but instead, he remained focused on the item he had just set down. "Here, take a look."

Marie looked at David's eyes.

"Go ahead. Look at it."

She knelt down and reached out to remove the cloth that covered the surprise. As the fabric slid away, it revealed a beautiful stone with words etched in its face. Marie read the inscription to herself, and David watched her face as tears welled up in her eyes.

After glancing back at him again, she returned her gaze upon the words and read aloud, "With unceasing love and humble adoration, I name this overlook Marie's Watch. I dedicate it to Marie Tudor, whose unselfish vision and hard work will benefit many who visit the Foxglove Inn." She reached out and caressed the etched letters. "Your signature and today's date are written as well. Thank you."

David smiled at her and felt happy this brought such emotion from her. It wasn't his original plan, as he had said, but it certainly was important to give credit where credit was due. This special day would forever be etched, not only in his mind, but on this stone, in history. Both of their names shared space on it. He liked that.

"Marie, are you hungry?" David tried to lighten the atmosphere. "Sheila made us lunch. Let's sit and enjoy it."

Rolling over to sit, Marie wrapped her arms around her knees. "David, this is so special. Thank you."

CHAPTER

21

Marie's heart was full. She sat beside David, looking out at the most beautiful scenery around them. The view of the inn and the village beyond was astounding. She chewed her lunch slowly as she took it all in. She would be enjoying this view often as part of her new job. She got butterflies as she thought about that.

So much had changed in her life recently, and that was all thanks to the wonderful man sitting quietly beside her. He was giving but never seemed to expect anything in return. Her gaze left the hillside and turned to rest on him. She watched him as he ate quietly, seemingly deep in thought.

"David?" she asked.

"Hmm?" He turned his attention toward her.

"I think you're wonderful," she said as she smiled widely.

"Do you really?" he asked.

"I do." Marie's response was heartfelt. "You've done so much for me. Please know I'm thankful for all you do." She hesitated a moment as she thought, then resumed, "I'm thankful for who you are."

"What do you mean, who I am?" David asked.

"As a person, I mean. You're always kind and not just to me but to everyone. I'm lucky to have come to know you so well."

David put his bread down and got up. Marie watched him, worried that she was making him feel uncomfortable. He walked to the edge of the overlook and stood facing the scenery for a few minutes in silence.

"You know you didn't have to do all this for me, the flowers, the stone, and the car," Marie said as she watched his back.

David bent down and picked up one of the groupings of roses, stood again, and turned back toward Marie. "I know I didn't have to do any of this, I wanted to."

He walked back to stand over her. Marie put her apple down and squinted through the bright sun as she looked up at him. She reached to shadow her eyes from the brightness that surrounded David.

"That's what I love about you, David." She heard her own words as they slipped out, and butterflies hit just as quickly. Those words were leading to something else, but suddenly, that was all that was hanging out there in the air.

He stepped out of the direct sun and knelt down on one knee beside her. He held up the bouquet of roses. "You see these, Marie?"

"Yes, they're beautiful."

"Yes, they are. But they're not nearly as beautiful as you are, both inside and out. You're a wonderful person, and I feel blessed for knowing you. In fact, I couldn't imagine not having you in my life."

David put the flowers down and fumbled around their stems, taking something out that had been hidden.

"Marie, I think about you all the time."

She sat even more erect; her heart started racing at his words.

He reached down and gently took Marie's hand in his. He caressed it briefly with his thumb and then held it higher as he exposed the ring from his other hand.

"Marie, will you marry me?"

She turned her body to face David straight on and looked in disbelief at the engagement ring he held over her fingers. His touch was electric and sent waves of chills through her very soul.

Before she could control her emotions, tears welled up in her eyes and spilled down her cheeks.

A look of concern replaced David's look of adoration. "Oh my goodness, Marie, are you okay?"

It felt as though David was about to release her hand, so she brought her other hand up to grasp his, but she couldn't find her voice. She nodded, offering silent assurance that she was fine, yet the tears kept coming. She tried taking deep breaths and blinking hard to clear her eyes so she could refocus on his face. His smile returned as she finally succeeded in bringing a shaky smile to her own quivering lips.

"We're so good together. I want to take care of you. I want to share my life with you. Will you be my wife?"

Though her emotions threatened to overtake her once more, she closed her eyes briefly, took a deep breath, and absorbed what was happening. Parting her lips, she released the last bit of shock and slowly opened her eyes to gaze into David's. It didn't take any amount of thinking to answer the most surprising question she had ever been asked.

"Yes, I will."

He gently slid the ring onto her finger. Then, leaning forward over his knee, he brought her chin up with one finger and kissed her quivering lips. He slipped to his spot beside her and wiped the wetness from her cheeks.

She could not stop looking at him. Only briefly could she take an occasional glance at the ring now adorning her finger. They had recently had a conversation about marriage. She knew how strongly he felt about it. Her mind was racing with the magnitude of his action.

"David?"

"Yes, dear?"

Chills ran down her spine with those endearing words. "Are you sure?"

He rose up a little straighter as he looked at her.

"I mean, I thought you were going to offer me a job today."

He laughed. "I know you would make a great employee, but honestly, I've had a different hope for a long time. You can still work if you want to, but you wouldn't be working for me."

"Wait a minute." Marie felt confused. "What do you mean?"

"The inn will be yours too. We'll be married. If you choose to work at the inn, which you don't have to, you'll be working for yourself."

"Oh. Oh my goodness. David, this is something you've worked so hard on. That doesn't sound right."

"My dear, you've become just as vested in it as I've been. I know that you only want what's best for our guests."

Our guests. The reality of the moment was sinking in but only slightly. "Oh my goodness, I can't believe this is happening to me!" Marie held her hand out in front of her to look at the proof of David's proposal. She turned toward him again, excitement racing through her.

"I love you, Marie."

She smiled and responded, "I love you, David."

"I have for a long time, you know."

Marie shook her head in disbelief. "I didn't know. I've felt it for a while now myself, but—" Marie hesitated. "I just can't believe this."

"I wasn't sure, with our age difference, if this was the right thing to do, but as I said, I can't imagine life without you, and with you graduated now, all grown up, the owner of a cute car, and free to move on in life, I had to face the reality that you might not stay here. I realized that I just had to ask."

"Our age difference? I don't think about it."

"I appreciate that, but I didn't want you strapped with an old man some day or miss out on meeting someone your own age that you might be happy with."

"I can't imagine getting close to anyone else, David. You really understand me." Marie became quiet briefly. "I can't wait to tell my parents!"

"I hope you don't mind," David said. "I already asked their permission. Your father and I've been friends since you were a little girl. I wouldn't have proposed if it meant hard feelings."

"So, they're happy?" she asked.

"It seemed so to me. They sounded very supportive."

Marie sat back and thought on the past few days. "I understand now. My mother couldn't sleep this morning either."

"Oh no," David said.

"No, I think it was good. She seemed excited for me and my future. It all makes sense now." Marie picked up her apple to finish her lunch, and David joined her, stretching out on the rock beside her.

When they were done, David folded his hands behind his head and watched the clouds fleeting across the blue sky. "What a great day."

Marie looked down at her future husband. The thought sent chills through her once more. "It is a great day, thanks to you."

David looked at her. "No, thanks to you."

"Why thanks to me? Look at all you did." Marie gestured to the flowers and the etched stone and then held her hand out once more to gaze upon its symbolism as she smiled.

"No," he said, "thanks to you. Could you imagine how awkward we would be feeling right now if you'd said no?"

CHAPTER

22

"Never could I have turned your proposal down." She looked back to him as he lay on the overlook beside her. "I love you and will forever."

He looked at her then rolled himself up to gently kiss her again, causing the butterflies to rise within her stomach.

"Okay, shall we set the date, then?" David asked, settling back to watch the clouds.

"Oh my goodness," Marie said. "I can't believe how much my life is changing. Okay, let's talk about a date. Did you have something in mind since you've been thinking about this so much?" She smiled at him.

"Well, as a matter of fact, I was thinking about next month."

"Next month?" she asked in surprise.

David glanced at her. "Is that too soon?"

"No. No, it's just soon."

David chuckled. "Too soon?"

"No. Not too soon, it's just soon. Does it take long to plan a wedding?"

"I suppose that depends on what kind of a wedding you want. What do you picture? Don't most girls have a fantasy of what their dream wedding would be like? What does yours look like?"

"Well, I suppose they do, but I'm not necessarily like most girls."

"No, I suppose you're not. That's why I love you so much. You're different. You're just right, just right for me."

Marie wasn't sure if that was really a compliment but decided to take it as one. "I don't know, David. I'm not fancy, and I don't really have friends that I'd invite." She looked at him to watch his reaction as she continued her thoughts. "I could envision it being small. Why not have it with my parents and your employees? They've all been supportive of you."

David smiled as he was listening. "And where would you like to have it?" he asked.

Marie was about to answer when he stopped her. "Wait, let me answer that, you'd like it in the field."

"Okay, smarty pants, is that what you want?" she asked.

"Since I'd already guessed correctly at how big you might want it, I thought I'd try my luck again. Was I right?"

She wanted David to be happy and enjoy the wedding of his dreams. After all, he was the one who waited until later in life when he felt it was the right person and the right time. "If you'd like it in the field, that'd be fine, but," she said, pointing, "I was just looking at the inn, remembering our dances on the terrace."

David sat up and looked down at the inn. "That's a fantastic idea! I wish I'd thought of that myself. I should've known."

"Okay, day or night?" she asked.

"That's an interesting question. I would assume day, but the inn is beautiful at night," he mused.

"I guess that means we both want it here and not somewhere else," Marie pointed out.

"Funny." David nodded. "It just seems natural to envision our wedding here at the inn."

"We could have an early evening ceremony while it's still daylight, small but simple on the terrace, and have a band for dancing later in the evening that we can invite the public to."

"That does sound like us." He smiled at her.

They continued planning and chatting deep into the afternoon before they decided to head back to the inn to share their news.

The wedding was simple yet elegant. Marie wore a lacy wedding gown, which had a dropped waist and a straight skirt that stopped just below the knee, following the latest fashion trend. The veil attached to a beautiful silk and lace cloche hat. It had a train that also attached, which trailed the ground behind Marie as she walked to the steady beat of the wedding march through the great room with her father at her side.

The guests seated on either side of the room were made up of a mixture of locals, political acquaintances of David's, entertainment personalities, and regular guests of the Foxglove Inn, those who could make it on short notice.

Marie stepped up the stairs and continued out the open French doors to David, who was waiting to receive her on the terrace. A much larger group of guests were seated on the lawn.

Since Scott was giving Marie away, Cam Morrison stood as David's best man. Marie smiled at Cam in appreciation. The decorations notably transformed the terrace, which caught Marie's eye right away. She took it all in and thought about how busy the staff had been and how appreciated they were. They were seated on the lawn in the front row, smiling at her. She glanced around as Pastor Dean asked who would give the bride away. She saw her mother seated on the terrace, looking beautiful and dabbing her eyes with her hankie. Marie winked at her. Her father lifted the veil to expose her face and kissed her cheek before leaving her side.

David stepped to the spot vacated by her father, symbolizing the transfer of responsibility for Marie's care. They looked into each other's eyes, and the feeling Marie experienced was nothing short of magic. They listened as Pastor Dean spoke of the memories he had of these two fine members of Roxboro's community, the changes David had made in the town, the love everyone had for them, and the God-given connection the couple seemed to share.

They faced each other as they repeated their vows, and though there were many people around them, Marie could only see David. She was excited to start her life with him. She thought of what a kind and compassionate man he was and squeezed his hand in hers. Her mind filled with the blessing of him when Pastor Dean finally declared them married and introduced them as husband and wife, Mr. and Mrs. Towell.

She felt honor in that moment. His name was one she would bear proudly. The wedding itself was a testimony to the man she was going to spend the rest of her life with. They had decided on a small wedding, but so many people loved him and wanted to be a part of it. He had made an impact in many lives. They may not have had close friends, but Marie suggested they all experience this joy with them.

Marie turned and threw her bridal bouquet high in the air so it would fall within the crowd on the lawn. She looked up at David, took his arm, and smiled when she heard the cheers. The wedding march resumed, indicating their expected return back through the inn. They walked through the open French doors together and into the great room to the cheering crowd inside and continued through the front entryway to a new door near David's office. It had a handmade sign on it that read, "Just Married." This new door led to a second floor that housed a suite, their suite, their new home.

With all the upgrades Marie's father had been working on, she wondered if he had been aware, when he first began it many months earlier, that this was going to be for her. Her father had built her a new home, and she was looking forward to seeing it for the first time. Her parents and David had furnished it, and

Marie's mother had prepared it with all the comforts of home that Marie was used to, so when she entered on this day she would want for nothing.

CHAPTER

23

It was June 13, 1927, the two-year anniversary of Marie's school graduation ceremony, and much had changed in this short time, David thought as he paced the hall outside their bedroom. The baby was coming, and though they felt prepared, he was a wreck. His sweet wife was in pain, a pain he couldn't help relieve. Only God could, and that was going to come with time, his time.

"Dear Father, please comfort Marie. I pray for your safety for both her and this child you are blessing us with as she prepares to deliver."

He heard Marie moan through the door again, and it brought cold sweat to his back.

"Father, help us all get through this time of labor. I know things are often far worse before they get better. I love her, and it's hard to hear her suffering."

David could hear Dr. Morse and Clara talking though it was muffled by the door. He resumed his pacing.

Scott appeared from downstairs and caught the tail end of David's prayer. "Then don't listen," he said. "Why don't you come downstairs with me? There's nothing you can do from out here."

"Scott, how can you be so calm? It's your daughter in there. She's suffering."

"Suffering? No more than a million other women who deliver babies," he retorted.

David could hear the sarcasm in his voice and scowled at him.

"I'm worried too, but I'm more excited than anything. I'm gonna be a grandpa!"

"Grandpa." David chuckled. "Makes you sound old, my friend."

"Funny, David." Scott's smile faded briefly. "Come on." He took him by the arm and led him to the stairwell. "Marie's in good hands."

David followed, leaving the suite he had Scott build above the offices of the inn for his new and growing family. There had been so much excitement in little more than two years in his life. He was grateful to God for the joy.

When they reached the great room, David headed to the terrace, where he sat down, happy there were no guests relaxing there, and resumed his praying, head bowed in his hands. This was his favorite place to sit as he could easily conjure up the memories of their wedding day while here. His bride had been absolutely beautiful.

David had not seen her the few days leading up to their wedding. "Absence makes the heart grow fonder," she had stated, but his heart would always remain fond of her regardless of proximity. They were meant to be together, of that he was sure.

He stood on the deck that day dressed in his one good suit, the same one he wore on opening day. The French doors were open with a white runner leading from the start of the great room all the way to where David had stood. It was through the open door that he had seen her appear like an angel dressed in a white wedding gown draped with lace. Her hair had been pulled up and was covered by a hat with a small veil obscuring part of her face, leaving her full lips exposed. She looked stunning.

He was remembering this vision now as he sat on the deck, giving thanks and praying for strength. Marie's pregnancy should not have taken them by surprise, but they were busy enjoying their life together, both fully involved with the business of the inn, that they hadn't thought about it. It was a happy surprise nonetheless, and she was radiant in her pregnancy, even when clumsiness took over. They had many moments to laugh at as her midsection became overwhelming.

The years' memories were flitting around his mind when a new sound reached his ears. He sat upright quickly and waited, listening intently for that sound once more to be sure his mind wasn't playing tricks on him. Scott was heading through the door with a glass of water for David when the sound pierced the air again. He bolted, knocking Scott against the French glass door he'd just opened causing him to spill some of the water as he ran by, through the great room, through the door by his office, and up the stairs.

He took the steps two at a time and felt the tears stinging his eyes even before he reached the door to their suite. The anticipation he was feeling was great. The love for his newborn child that he'd not even met yet overwhelmed him, and the concern for his wife's comfort was deeply embedded. It was all so much for him to have been holding in for the past nine hours since Marie had gone into labor. He threw the door open and nearly ran into his mother-in-law, who was reaching for the doorknob.

"I was just coming to get you," she said.

It was as if he didn't see or hear Clara. He rushed right to their bedroom door and stopped, his emotions showing on his face. "Marie? Are you okay?"

Marie was propped up on the bed and looked up from the baby she was holding swaddled in her arms. "Oh David, come here."

He tentatively took a couple of steps forward.

"Come, come," Marie said as she patted the bed beside her.

David closed the space between them quickly and gently slid onto the bed beside her, leaned in close, and kissed her forehead before his eyes followed the direction she was looking, into the beautiful eyes of their newborn child.

"Marie?"

"David, meet your daughter Abigail."

"Abigail. It's a girl?" David asked. He had been open and excited for whatever God had planned for them, but hadn't really thought about it until this minute. "A girl. Marie, she's a girl!"

Marie smiled. "Yes, a girl."

"Abigail. Oh my." David bent down and kissed his daughter ever so gently on her head. "She's beautiful, honey." Tears slipped down his cheeks.

Marie looked surprised. "David, are you happy?"

"Oh, Marie, I'm happy, I'm relieved, I'm excited, and I'm scared. I was so worried about you. How are you feeling?" he asked.

She laughed as she echoed his answer, "Tired, but happy, relieved, excited, and scared." She leaned her head to rest on her husband's arm, gazed down at their daughter, and sighed. "We're parents."

David snuggled in deeper, and the three remained in bed for hours. As Marie and David cuddled and caressed Abigail, the world went on around them. They barely noticed when Clara brought a meal up and left it on the bureau. The sound of laughter drifted in at times through the open window. The summer season was just starting to gear up, and some families had come early to enjoy a less busy time at the inn. The faint sound of horses whinnying reached their ears.

"I feel so full, Marie." David's finger was being gripped by his new child, and his head was propped up next to his wife's. "God has been so good to me."

"Do you really think so?" she asked.

"Don't you?" David asked in surprise. "He led me to ask you to marry me. I wouldn't have done it without his direction."

Marie stiffened a bit in response. "You didn't want to marry me?"

David looked to his wife, who seemed hurt, and he chuckled. "I can hear how that sounded, but that's not what I meant."

"Okay, I'm listening."

"I was close friends with your dad. We built this place when you were turning nine. I'm almost old enough to be your father, after all, but when you came back to Roxboro, we spent more and more time with each other. I was comfortable with you."

Marie smiled and snuggled close. "Of course."

"Well, as you were getting closer to graduation, I thought of us in a different way."

Marie reached up and caressed David's face as if in teasing. "A different way?"

"Okay, it wasn't that easy then. I felt like it was wrong. As I've told you, I didn't want to upset your life, but I was falling in love with you. I would think of you often and wondered what life might be like if you moved away after graduation. So, I asked God what I should do. If it was not right that we be together, I prayed for strength to let go of you, but I wanted a clear sign if I was to ask you to be my wife."

Marie was listening intently now. "You asked for guidance about me?"

"You know how I felt about marriage. I didn't want to be unhappy in one or to have someone unhappy and feeling stuck with me."

"Who could be unhappy with you?" she asked.

"Well, I know God has a plan for my life, and I only want what he wants for me. If you were meant to be with me and marriage was intended for us, God would let me know."

"How? How could he possible tell you to marry me?"

"I put out a fleece."

"What does that mean, put out a fleece?"

As they picked at the food that had been waiting for them, David shared the Bible story from the book of Judges. He told of Gideon's request for assurance from God and how he used a fleece in seeking it.

After she heard the whole story, she asked, "So, what was the fleece you put out about me? You've got me awfully interested now."

"Well, one day I asked him, 'I'm going to look for a place that'll be special for me and Marie, where I could propose to her. But, I don't want to keep focusing on her if we're not meant to be together. If I'm supposed to propose, show me with a dance.'"

"A dance? You were uncomfortable dancing. Why would you have asked that?"

David caressed her arm and kissed Abigail's head. "That word just came to mind, but I realized that's what would've made it clear, because it was unlikely."

"It sounds like you made it difficult, like you didn't want it to be true."

"Now, Marie, if you're asking God to make something clear, you can't set his answer up so it will likely happen. Then you'd never know if he really was in it. When the answer could've only come from him, that's when you know for sure, just like Gideon."

"Yeah, you just explained that he asked God twice for confirmation. So, what happened next?"

"A rock fell on me."

Marie started laughing, which made Abigail squirm and whimper. "Shh, honey. It's okay." Marie kissed her daughter's cheek and nestled her a little closer. She looked at David. "Wait a minute, at the overlook?"

"Yes, Marie, and what came over you to take advantage of an injured man and blackmail him?"

Marie's eyes grew wide with realization as she whispered in amazement, "A dance."

"Not just one dance," David pointed out. "But a dance every week. I set out a fleece asking for something so improbable, to be sure we wouldn't end up unhappy. I wanted to be absolutely sure it was God's plan and not mine. So, he pinned me under a rock so you could laugh at me and bargain my life for a dance." David laughed as chills ran down his spine. "A dance every week."

CHAPTER

24

Marie was a very good mother, and Abigail was growing fast. Life at the inn had been good for them, but David was anxious for a new adventure.

"If we sell now, I'm sure we'd have quite a lot to invest."

Marie was supportive of the changes he was suggesting for their family. "This sounds exciting, David." She reached out to steady Abigail, who was cruising around the coffee table, holding on tightly as her pudgy legs took unsteady steps. "I'll miss my parents, though."

"Well, with the transportation systems as good as they are now, we can visit them easily enough. We could even stay here at the inn when we come visit."

Marie chuckled at the thought. "Wouldn't that feel strange?" Abigail reached out and grasped Marie's pant leg, continuing her journey along her mother's side, mumbling sounds as she went.

"I wonder what'll change after we leave," David mused.

"When will you talk with our employees?"

"I'm meeting with the realtor tomorrow, so I thought I'd call a staff meeting Tuesday morning." David walked to Marie's side and bent down to pick Abigail up. "What do you think, honey?" he asked his daughter as he held her high in the air. She squealed with excitement, kicking her feet. "Are you ready for a new adventure?"

"Do you think we could bring Duplin with us? I'd like to ride again now that Abigail's getting older. She loves the horses just as much as I do."

"We could look for a property with some land and a barn."

"However, if you're going to be busy traveling, perhaps it wouldn't be a good idea," Marie pointed out.

David sat down on the loveseat next to Marie. Abigail climbed over to her mother, where she stood on her lap and hugged her face. Marie chuckled, kissing her baby's neck.

"I think we can hire someone to take care of a barn for us. That way you won't have your hands too full." He looked at Marie and watched as she and Abigail played. Even though he was excited for their new plans, he was worried. "What if we're making the wrong choice in leaving?"

"Now, David, how can you ask that? It was you, after all, that taught me to trust God. We put a fleece out, and he answered it. Let's step forward trusting, not looking back. Have a little faith, my love. God has a plan and obviously needs you somewhere else." She smiled slyly at him.

"I love you, Marie. God could not have given me a better wife." He leaned over and embraced both of his girls, planting kisses on each. "Are you ladies up for a walk?"

"Can we go to the barn?" Marie asked cheerfully.

"Of course." David picked their daughter up, and the three headed out of the suite.

Chance picked his head up as the door was opening and ran to catch up.

"Okay, boy, let's go."

The family left the quiet of their home and entered the busy atmosphere of the inn. Business had been good, and many families were returning, prompting them to build additional buildings. David and Scott had worked up plans for seven small bungalows with large covered porches, each with three small bedrooms, a bath, and a common area. They were being built on the outskirts of the large field, and it appeared as though they were going to be done on schedule. In time for the upcoming summer months.

David and Marie wandered hand in hand up the path to the barn. Abigail began acting excited, rocking in her daddy's arms and reaching toward the paddock, where a few horses where grazing.

"Duplin!"

The horse raised his head as Marie's voice drifted across the wind. He whinnied, reached down for another bite, then turned and trotted toward them.

David positioned Abigail on the top rail so she could face the pasture while he held her from behind. Marie reached down and grasped a handful of clover, stepped on the lower rail, and hung over the top, extending her hand toward Duplin, who picked up his pace. Marie watched her daughter's face. She was having difficulty containing her excitement as the horse reached them. He took the grass that was extended to him as Marie rubbed his head.

"Hey, boy, good boy," Marie mumbled in affection as he brought his head over the railing between Marie and David.

David held Abigail tighter as she reached out to grab at Duplin.

"Good boy, Duplin," Marie said soothingly to distract him from the excitement that was coming from the other side. She laughed as she held his halter. "Good boy."

David picked Abigail up and held her closer to Duplin's neck. "Here you go, honey." He held one of her hands and helped her to stroke his neck. "This is how you pat the horsey."

Marie chuckled as she nuzzled the other side of his neck.

"What's so funny?" David asked.

"You're such a good dad. It's cute."

"You think so? I'm cute, huh?" he asked.

"Well, you are, but I said *it's* cute, as in it's cute to listen to you with her," she responded.

"Marie, come look at Abigail."

She stepped back and around Duplin. "Oh, honey. You love Duplin too?"

Abigail had laid her head against his neck, and the look on her face was one of pure bliss.

"Nice horsey," David said softly as he patted Duplin with her hand.

Duplin stepped away and trotted back out to the pasture, leaving the three behind; he'd had enough of their affection. They turned and looked down the hill at the inn, the life they were planning to leave.

David put his arm around Marie's shoulder. "What do you think, honey?"

She took a deep breath. "I think I'm excited," she answered.

He had mixed feelings. This new life as a husband and father meant more to him than he could have ever imagined. He had enjoyed change and moving from experience to experience earlier in his life, but now things were different. Being a family man brought him great joy, and he had taken the responsibility very seriously. He also loved the feeling of being settled, but now change was calling once more, causing him to feel a bit apprehensive. He looked out over all the inn had become. Then he looked down at his wife beside him and felt chills pass through him. He was happy to have her support as they prepared to transition and felt blessed for who she was and the faith they had come to share. God's direction was clear; they were to head east, but no other details were known.

Marie looked up and smiled at him, then took Abigail's hand and kissed it. She giggled that little girl giggle that David found so endearing.

"Wanna go see some more horses?" Marie asked her daughter.

Abigail responded by moving back and forth.

David laughed. "She's trying to get me going."

"Let's go up to the barn, honey. We'll see some more horses."

Abigail's sounds that she excitedly sputtered seemed much like words at times, and this time, it caused her parents to look at each other in amazement.

"Did you hear it?" David asked.

"I think so," Marie responded. "Horses," Marie stated slowly and clearly to her daughter, who started bucking in movement again as if to get them moving. She sputtered the same sound again.

"Horse! Horse! I heard it. David, she said horse!"

"Horse," David repeated slowly to his daughter.

They continued coaching her new word as they hiked the rest of the way to the barn. When they entered, a group of guests had just returned from a trail ride. David and Marie brought Abigail to a pony in a stall near the door so they could stay out of the way.

David overheard the excitement of a guest in the crowd. "The view from Marie's Watch was simply beautiful," she said.

"Matter o' fact, that's Marie right there," Charlie responded.

David turned his head to see him pointing them out.

"And that's her husband, David Towell." Charlie waved to David as he continued. "He's the owner and the guy that dedicated the overlook. Story is, he dedicated the overlook just before he proposed." David saw the wink directed at him.

He turned back to his family, who hadn't seemed to notice the attention they were drawing.

Marie's Watch had been visited regularly by their guests ever since it was the setting of the most important day of his life. He realized now that it made great conversation. It really was a romantic story. He smiled as he reached out to rub his wife's back.

CHAPTER

25

Over the summer, David and Marie entertained a number of prospective buyers. The meetings were bittersweet, and they eventually realized how difficult it was going to be to leave. Once Abigail was settled down for the night, they sat in the living room talking about their prospects.

"It'll be winter before we know it. How much longer should we wait?" Marie asked.

"It was just business to him. I could tell," David mused about Mr. Thurston, who'd just spent a week with them. "I don't think he really had a feeling for this place."

"I have to agree with you this time, David," Marie said. "This is too important to sell it to someone who's only looking at the money."

"Our employees are family. They helped build this place. They've raised their children while working here."

"I grew up here," Marie added, "to some degree." The smile on her face was shy but telling.

David chuckled at her look. "Well, what about the Spencer family?"

Dick and Stella Spencer came for three days in early July. They were thorough in their analysis of the buildings, grounds, and staff. They asked a lot of questions and seemed very serious as they researched what it would take to run an inn.

"I liked them well enough," Marie said. "I don't know. There was something odd about them."

"I know what you mean, but I couldn't put my finger on it."

Marie smiled. "What are we looking for anyway? Who are we waiting for? We are moving on to another adventure, aren't we?"

"We are," he answered.

"What are we waiting for, then, David?"

He turned toward Marie. "I don't know. I think God will show us who's right. This is important. I didn't just build this business and help this town to hand it over to someone who doesn't mean to care for it, love the people, and give it all it deserves. I really think we'll know it when we see it."

"It? You mean them, don't you?"

David stood and walked to the window to look out over the back lawn and the pasture on the hill. He turned back toward Marie. "I mean, look at this. Look at the beauty around us. I'm looking for a steward, someone to nurture it, not just for the money, someone who'll love it as we have."

Marie joined her husband. They looked out the window together. "I'm glad you feel that way. I feel the same, and I'm sure we'll find it. Let's stop worrying and leave it in God's hands. You're right, he'll let us know."

David turned toward her, looking excited. "Marie, let's take the horses out tomorrow. I want to go up to Marie's Watch, just you and me. Trisha can watch Abigail."

Marie looked back out the window. "I haven't been up there since I found out I was pregnant."

"I know. Well, what do you think?" He looked longingly at her, making sure the over dramatization of his look was noticed. "I'll bring a picnic lunch. Just like old times, right? Let's make it a date." He got down on one knee and took Marie's hand in his. "Marie, will you go on a date with me tomorrow?"

She chuckled. "Oh David, that'd be great. I think I'd rather ask my mom to watch Abigail, though. Would you mind?"

"Of course I don't mind. I'll call her now, before it gets too late."

David left the suite, feeling excited. A date, they had not spent a day away from the inn alone together since Abigail was born. Family life was great, David had no complaints there, but he and Marie really needed time alone together. Actually, he realized, Marie needed and deserved some time to not be taking care of something or someone else, to be the focus of attention for a change.

After calling Clara, who was excited to take care of her granddaughter, David went to the kitchen to explain his plans. When morning arrived, he slipped away quietly and headed to town without mentioning to Marie that he was leaving; he had some work to do before their date.

Just before eleven when Clara arrived, David ran up to the barn for the final touches. He waited for the signal from his mother-in-law. Charlie helped him saddle the horses, and he stood with Duplin's reins in one hand and Storm's in the other. The wait seemed endless before he saw a hankie hanging out of the window.

He walked the horses down to the inn. "Marie!" he hollered.

In a few moments, the window opened, and his wife popped her head out. A big smile found its place on her face. "David, what's this?"

"Your chariot awaits, my dear. Come, let me take you away."

Duplin shook his head and snorted, causing the flowers that were tucked throughout his mane to be disturbed. He leaned down to pick a rose up off the ground and could hear Marie laughing. He returned it to its place.

"Are you coming?" he asked.

"I'll be right down. Hold on a minute."

David began readjusting the flowers when he heard Marie's voice from above. She had picked Abigail up to see the horses.

"Horsey, horsey." Abigail's words were much clearer now at a year old. "Daddy, horsey."

"Yes, honey, horsey." Marie responded. "Here." Marie's words faded as she turned away from the window with Abigail.

David waited, though it didn't take long before his wife stepped out onto the terrace and walked over to meet him. He moved Duplin up alongside the stairs so Marie could easily step into the stirrup. "Ready, my dear?"

Marie climbed on and took a deep breath. "I guess I am."

David mounted Storm and rode up alongside his date.

"I thought this'd feel foreign, getting back in the saddle," Marie said. "It feels like I just rode him yesterday." She reached down and caressed Duplin's neck.

David caught her eye and was transported back in time. He remembered that feeling of being in love but not being sure he should expose that truth. He remembered how perfect she was for him and the deep sadness at the chance he would not be beside her one day. His heart filled, once again, with that feeling of young, excited love.

"What are you smiling at, David?" Marie's voice was soft. "You keep looking at me."

"You're beautiful, Marie," he said.

She turned away, that shy girl once more. "Well, thank you, kind sir."

They enjoyed spending time in conversation as they rode slowly through the field.

"Do you suppose we should find a home in a city, Marie? A quiet town or perhaps one on the ocean? Our future is wide open. Where have you ever dreamed you could spend your days?" David asked.

They had agreed that David's next business, whatever God directed it to be, should be separate from their home. This would allow David the ability to focus on work when he was there and on his family when he was with them. This meant that their home location options were rather open.

Marie turned her attention back to her husband. "I've often wondered what city living would be like, right in the middle of all the chaos, but I'm not really a city kind of girl. My choice would be the ocean, I think."

They continued riding toward the trail.

"David, could you picture us riding the horses on a beach? Doesn't that just sound like a romantic fantasy? Imagine my hair whipping in the ocean breeze as we race. I bet I could beat you, just like this!"

Marie kicked her heels into Duplin's sides, causing him to jump forward and begin racing away. David was caught by surprise and fondly remembered the spunky girl she'd been only a few years earlier.

"Come on, Storm. Let's catch up." He dug his heels in as well and joined the chase until they came to the pull off.

"It's about time you showed up," Marie said with a smile. She was already dismounting when David arrived.

He got down, tied up his horse, and took their luncheon satchel out of his saddlebag. "I was just taking a relaxing ride. I'm not in a rush to get through our date." He winked at Marie.

"Hey, I'm not trying to rush our time together!" She walked up to him, rose to her tippy toes, and gave him a slow kiss. "I love you."

"I love you too."

The pair wandered together up the path they had created, and when they reached the rocks, David paused to let her go ahead of him.

Seconds later, Marie popped her head back around the rocks to look at him, just as she had the day he proposed.

"David, oh my goodness. This is beautiful." She reached out her hand for him to take, and they stepped out onto Marie's Watch together. "When did you do this?"

He looked around with a big grin on his face as he thought back to the day he had brought up the same type of flowers. He took her in his arms. "Marie, if I could, I'd marry you all over again. I want you to know how blessed I am that God brought you into my life. I want your life to be filled with flowers and that you'll always know that I love you when you see them."

CHAPTER

26

The winter had been mild but long, and now that it was coming to a close, the warmer air brought those suffering from spring fever some degree of relief. At just over a year and a half now, Abigail was quite the handful. The staff were tolerant of her mischief. She loved to bang on the pots, pull on anything that hung over a table edge, and she figured out how to get out a door quicker than her mother could chase her.

David came into their suite and found Marie spread out on the couch, looking exhausted. "Hi, honey," he said when she looked his way.

Marie jerked up to a sitting position and threw her finger to her mouth in a desperate attempt to insist on quiet. She glanced toward Abigail's room.

David smiled, leaned down, kissed his frazzled wife on the forehead, and then whispered, "We'll own the oceanfront house next Friday. Wait, isn't that your twenty-first birthday?"

This brought Marie to standing. "Oh my, really?" She caught herself and repeated in a whisper, "Oh my, really?"

David hugged her weary body and whispered in her ear, "Happy birthday. We close on the house on Minnesott Beach next Friday, March twenty-third." He held her hands as they sank to the couch together.

"We haven't accepted a buyer for the inn yet, David. Aren't you concerned about that?" Marie asked in a hushed voice.

They talked quietly so as not to wake the napping busybody.

"I'm not concerned. You know I've been saving money over the years to pay for something outright."

"I love that you do that. Everyone that I know buys on credit, except you. What made you decide to live like that?"

"I'm not sure really. At first it just happened. One small business led to enough money to start the next one. When I was growing up, my parents fought all the time. Besides fights about my dad's drinking, much of those arguments were about money. I never wanted to live feeling that kind of stress, and if debt contributed to it, then I didn't want any part of it."

"That sounds wise." Marie snuggled into his side.

David smiled down at her. It felt great having his wife close. "Well, since then I've come to realize it was God's will for me to live like this. When I was looking at this property, the big empty barn, I was visiting the church in town, and during one of the sermons, Pastor Dean quoted something from the Bible that really stood out to me. It went something like, 'Owe nothing to anyone except to love one another'. 'Owe nothing to anyone' stood out to me, loud and clear, because that's what I'd already felt. It was as if God had put it on my heart before I even knew him."

"So, we buy the house at the ocean with the money you've saved and start your next business with the money we earn from selling the inn?" she asked.

"That's what I'm planning, Lord willing. We're expecting the Tate's to come stay for a week in May. I met with them a couple of weeks ago. They have a lot of loose ends to tie up before they can seriously consider purchasing this, but I'm hopeful. They're dealing with debt and trying to figure out what they can afford to do."

"Don't we have someone coming next month too?" she asked.

"Yeah, a businessman named Patrick Dorsey. He's not staying, though, just checking us out for a day. He's bringing his lawyer with him. I guess I hadn't really put much thought into him. I've always spent time in an investment decision getting to know the people and the place. I don't think his intentions are more than a business transaction. I don't believe he's the guy for us." David couldn't imagine this being God's will. "I was hoping for a family."

"Sounds like I'm not interested in even meeting him. I think Abigail and I have to go shopping that day or something," Marie responded with a giggle.

"Well, you don't have to be here. You'll have a house at the ocean to live in."

She smiled, but the smile faded.

"What is it, honey?" David asked.

"It's going to feel odd, us not being together all the time."

"I'll stay there with you on weekends after we get you settled in." He hugged her reassuringly. "Don't worry, Marie. It'll be fine. We plan on doing this when I start a new business anyway, so this'll be the practice."

She turned toward him just as Abigail's voice pierced the quiet of the room. "Daddy!"

Marie closed her eyes and took a deep breath. "I'm not going to worry, David. God has been good to us, and I trust him. I'm thankful for the new house and really, really excited. That's got to be the best birthday present ever!"

"Wait a minute," David responded, "I thought Duplin was the best present ever, or was it the car?"

Marie laughed. "Okay, a house on the beach isn't a big deal. I just didn't want you to feel bad." She winked at him as she stood to get Abigail.

David stood, intercepting her movement. He took his wife in his arms. "I don't look forward to being apart either. Hey, why don't we ask your mother to stay with you at the ocean until I get the inn under contract?"

"Do you think she would?" Marie asked. "Oh, that'd be wonderful. Maybe Daddy could stay too. Maybe for a week or so at least. I'd love that."

"I would too." David was worried about his sweet Marie. As much as she seemed strong and independent, her insecurities were starting to stand out a bit more lately. She seemed, at times, as though she didn't know what to do next. It was subtle, but it nagged at David. He wasn't quite sure, but there was something different about her.

He put his finger to his mouth and then released Marie. Turning from her, he stepped quietly to the edge of Abigail's doorway and slowly peeked around the corner. She was lying in her crib, looking at her hands, chatting.

"Sweetie," David called to her quietly. His voice didn't break her focus.

She didn't notice him until he stepped closer. "Daddy," she said as she stood for him to take her out of her confinement.

David leaned down, kissed the top of her head, then hugged her. "I love you, Abigail."

He couldn't have imagined his life so full of all the blessings he lived with today. The investments, the businesses, the money were all meaningless. It was this love that life was for, true, deep, and unconditional.

He picked Abigail up and carried her back to the living room to join Marie. "You be a good girl, Abigail. Look, Mommy's all tired out because of you." He poked her belly as she giggled.

"I good girl," Abigail responded and wiggled to get down.

David sat down beside Marie and let Abigail shrug her way to the floor, where she wandered to the disheveled bookshelf that held all her books, blocks, and pull toys. She pulled down the basket of blocks, which sent them tumbling to the floor then sat happily in the midst of them.

Marie looked frustrated at the sound.

David put his hand on her knee and snuggled into her neck as he whispered, "Don't let it bother you, my dear."

"How can I not?" Her voice sounded defeated. "It's a full-time job following her around and cleaning up after her."

David sat up to look at her and suggested, "Then don't. Make it your full-time job to join her. She's only going to stay small for a short time. Enjoy it. Enjoy her."

"But things get messy so quickly."

"So what, I don't care if I'm stepping over blocks, because I know there's happiness tied to them." He kissed Marie's forehead and held both her hands. "Really Marie, I want you to pray for peace about this. You and Abigail have one relationship, and it'll always grow and change, but she will be this age"—he turned and looked at her as she played—"for such a short time. Relax. Please sit and be a part of it."

"Wouldn't you be upset living in a messy home?"

"Certainly not, and if your frustration is tied to the thought that I would judge you, then let me assure you, I want you free of that feeling. I love you. I love Abigail, and I want you two to be happy together. If something's irritating you, then I want you to pray for guidance and freedom from it."

Marie sat quietly as if pondering her husband's encouragement as he got up and went to sit on the floor beside their daughter. She turned and watched as the pair played together, building castles and bridges, breaking and rebuilding them at will.

David turned to see her watching. He patted a spot on the floor for her then pushed blocks out of the way so she could sit down. She sat between them, and the three of them built, destroyed, and laughed. He thought that perhaps Marie could sense the difference getting involved might make and was hopeful that her stress level might lessen.

"Okay, kids," she said, "what do you say we head down for some dinner?"

Abigail stood up and walked to the door.

David tugged at Marie's skirt and motioned for her to watch him. "Oh, Abigail, are you ready to eat?"

"Yup," she answered with her cute little girl voice.

"Well, before we eat, let's play one more game."

She turned back from the door to see what her daddy meant.

"Here, come and see."

She walked back to him curiously as he put the basket on the floor in front of the bookshelf.

"Watch Daddy," he said as he stepped back and tossed a block into the basket and announced, "One. Daddy got one block in the basket. You try now."

Abigail jumped up and down excitedly and grabbed a block for herself and threw it with poor aim and no luck.

Marie stifled a laugh and stepped forward. "Mommy's turn." She picked up a block and tossed it but only reached the side of the basket.

David assumed it was on purpose, but he continued with another block. Soon they had all the blocks picked up.

David lifted the basket back to the top of the bookshelf and reached for Abigail's hand. "Okay, Mommy. Let's go to dinner. I'm tired of playing."

She smiled at him as he offered her a wink of encouragement.

CHAPTER

27

David had risen to his knees so he could see those around him. "I want to thank you for coming here to celebrate Abigail's birthday," he said as his own laughter cut his words short.

Cameron Morrison; Marie's parents, Clara and Scott Tudor; and Charlie Procter, the stable hand from the inn, had all accepted the invitation to Abigail's party and joined them on the beach at their new house. David was travelling home each weekend to be with Marie and Abigail while staying at the inn during the week. Marie's father and Charlie travelled with him and were staying the weekend. Marie's mother had been staying with Marie at the beach house but was returning home with her husband at the end of this weekend.

"I could've found something less laborious to do had I known what the requirement would be in coming here," Cam mentioned from an awkward position on his knees.

"I agree! I don't have the imagination I thought I had either!" Scott hollered.

Clara started laughing from where she knelt as she looked up. "Abigail, I need more water over here!"

Abigail got off her perch where she was looking at a new picture book she had just unwrapped and ran with her pail to the ocean. "I get water, I get water." She kept repeating those words under her breath as she struggled to carry the small bucket of water back to her Grammy.

"Thank you, honey," Clara said as she took the bucket from her pudgy hands and filled the void in the sand that was meant to hold it.

"That ain't fair." Charlie's voice sounded muffled. "I don't get no help. David, why's Clara gettin' help?"

David popped his head up again from behind his pile of sand. "Yeah, I don't think that's fair either. This is a competition."

"Oh, stop your complaining!" Marie shouted. "Give the ladies a break. Abigail, I need some water too, honey."

Abigail turned from her grandmother's side, looked to her mother, then ran back to the water's edge.

Clara laughed loudly. "I'm all done anyway. I was just making the final touches."

Cam stood and stretched his arms up high. "I'm way too old for this. I can tell you that for sure. I'm gonna be lame for a week." After a few deep bends and a stretch to his neck, he returned to his knees and resumed his work.

Clara got up and walked around each of her competitor's sculptures and looked as though she was critically analyzing them. When she reached Marie, she took Abigail's hand. "Do you want to show me your picture book while Mommy's finishing?"

Abigail and her grandmother walked back to the beach chairs and sat down together.

David glanced up and watched Marie. She seemed deep in thought, watching her mother and daughter. He sat back on his heels in the sand, felt it squish between his toes, felt the coolness of the water soaking in, and looked up at their beautiful, new house. *Lord, you've led me through so many adventures and have increasingly impressed on me to trust and rely on you. Thank you for making this possible.*

His attention returned to Marie when he heard the words *unconditional love* clearly, as if they were spoken to him from behind. He continued watching his wife as he thought on God's words. He was sure that was why they were so good together. She loved him unconditionally. She always had. He believed he offered her the same.

"I'm done." Scott stood up from behind his mound of sand that had taken shape through the hour. "My back's aching now. Clara, I think I'm gonna need a massage before the day's out." He walked over and sat on the sand beside his wife's beach chair.

"Okay, we're down to four people workin'. Who's gonna finish next, I wonder," Charlie said before he stood up and wiped off his knees. "I know. It's me!"

Everybody laughed as he walked to an empty chair. "I thought the last one done automatically loses," Charlie hollered over his shoulder to the three who continued working.

"Hey!" David shouted. "I don't think so. Stop pressuring me."

"I'm done." Cam stood up and walked to the water's edge, waiting for the tide to cover his feet as he looked out over the ocean. After a few minutes, he turned around and looked at all the sand sculptures before walking back toward the group. "You know, those don't look half bad," he said.

"Okay," Marie spoke up, "I'm done too."

"No!" David's protest was loud.

Marie walked up to the sculpture her husband was working on. "You know what your problem is, David? You're too much of a perfectionist."

"Oh no, I'm not, my dear. You can't call me that just because I'm taking this competition seriously." He stood up and leaned frontward and backward getting the kinks out of his back. "You just wait and see who wins. Then you'll know that effort and technique, both of which take time, are worth it."

The crowd all laughed at his explanation.

"You just wait." David pointed his finger menacingly at the crowd before dropping back to his knees and picking up the stick he had been using to chisel the fine details of his creation.

"David, we're waiting. Hurry up," Marie said kiddingly. After a few minutes of watching him, she walked away, leaving him to painstakingly perfect his work.

Just after she sat down with their friends, he shouted, "There, I'm done!"

The crowd rose and cheered.

Marie leaned down to Abigail. "Okay, honey. For your birthday, each of us has created a sand gift for you. You must understand, though"—Marie got down to her level as she continued—"that they'll be erased by the ocean tonight. For now, it's your turn to be the judge. Can you choose the one you like the best?"

"Yup," Abigail answered.

"Now, I want you to walk around each of them and look really hard, and then let us know which one is your favorite," David explained.

"Okay," Abigail said. She wandered off as the group watched her.

"Oh, I forgot to mention," David whispered so Abigail couldn't hear, "the one who wins is the one who'll be putting the clown outfit on. It's in the spare bedroom, and the face paint's in the cupboard under the bathroom sink. Don't let her know who it is, though. She's going to love it."

"David, do you honestly think any of us want to dress up like a clown? That's the prize?" Marie spoke in shock on behalf of the whole group.

He looked at them incredulously. "You're kidding, right? Who wouldn't want to dress up like a clown for a two-year-old, little girl on her birthday? She's going to love it."

They all laughed at him.

"Well, I hope I win, then." With those final words, he turned to watch his daughter as she walked around the forms spread out on the beach.

"Daddy, what's this?" Abigail shouted to David. He went to stand with her as she looked at his creation.

"It's a mermaid, Abigail."

She looked at it again. "What's a mermaid, Daddy?"

David heard the chuckles of his friends and family as he explained to her what the character was.

"Oh, that sounds scary," Abigail said.

"No, honey," David answered. "Mermaids are magical, not scary."

"He's trying to sway her opinion." Cam's voice was heard loudly over the sound of the wind.

David waved his hand at his friend to suggest that he quiet down. "Honey, do you like it?" he asked.

Abigail looked out over the other sculptures and finally answered, "I like the mer, mer... Daddy, I don't remember. What's it called?"

David stood tall and spoke loudly, "Mermaid. You like Daddy's mermaid, honey? So, does that mean I'm the winner?"

She smiled up at him. "Daddy's the winner!"

David picked her up in his arms and tossed her up into the air and shouted in a sing-song voice, "Daddy's a winner, Daddy's a winner!"

Later, as everyone sat around the kitchen table getting ready to eat cake, David, who had excused himself to the restroom some time earlier, popped in fully decked out in clown attire. Big baggy outfit, oversized shoes, cone hat, red hair that stood out at least six inches on either side of his head, painted face, and a bright-red nose. He waddled in, trying to juggle and dropping balls as he went. By the time he reached Abigail, she was clinging tightly to her mother's leg.

"Mommy, I'm scared. Mommy! Mommy! Make it go away!" Abigail sunk her face into her mother's pant leg.

Marie picked Abigail up as she buried her face in her mother's shoulder, not daring to look up again. The entire crowd around the table laughed unstoppably, Clara nearly to tears. Marie did her best to console her daughter between fits of laughter. David left the room as quickly as he had come in.

CHAPTER

28

"I'm confused." David couldn't sleep and called Marie late at night to seek her counsel.

"David, you prayed about it." He could hear how sleepy she was, but he needed to hear her thoughts.

"I know," he answered, "but the answer I'm getting doesn't make sense."

"It doesn't make sense to you. Don't you think it does to God?"

"I just wish I knew for sure."

"David." Marie's voice became firmer. "You do know for sure. Just because you can't see what his plan is doesn't mean you're misunderstanding his direction. You've taught me that. Remember, trust and obey."

"For there's no other way," David continued the words from a song they knew from church. "I know you're tired. I'm sorry to bother you."

"You're never a bother."

Marie's answer made him miss her all the more. These long nights separate seemed more difficult than he had expected.

David had lost sleep the past three nights since Patrick Dorsey from Steward Enterprises, a large-scale holder of inns and hotels, had called with an offer. He and his lawyer had spent a very business-minded day analyzing the Foxglove Inn four months earlier in April. The first half of that day was focused on the buildings themselves. They checked them out thoroughly from top to bottom, both taking notes as they went. Mid to late afternoon was spent monitoring the staff, asking questions about their qualifications, and reviewing their personnel files. They ended the day perusing the books and the history of financials. It was intimidating.

"The Tate's were wonderful, Marie. They're a couple trying to move into something just like this. I could picture them loving what we built and continuing the atmosphere we've established."

"I understand your confusion, David. I think, though, that you have clear direction from God, and you need to just step out on faith and make it happen. Shake the man's hand just as you dreamt."

"What do I tell the Tate's, Marie? I really liked them, and they've tried so hard to get ready for this."

"The truth, tell them the truth. I know this is personal for you. You've worked hard creating the inn as you envisioned long ago, but it's God's. In this case, you must treat it as business. I know God's with you, David. I know you'll find the right way to let them know."

David could tell Marie was really tired. "Thank you, honey, for listening. You're right, and I do trust God. His direction's clear, and I pray that he forgives my hesitation to follow. I love you. I'll call you tomorrow."

David woke the next morning after a good night's sleep, refreshed and ready to tackle the next step in their lives. All he had to do was let go of control and trust God's odd direction. He called the Tate's first, and after explaining his decision, encouraged them to pray, something he wasn't even sure they believed in, and trust that God would give them direction that would be best for them.

He called Steward Enterprises next and accepted the offer they had placed on the inn. It was a few thousand dollars higher than he had been asking. They were obviously trying to sway him in their direction. They knew David had entertained many buyers but had hesitated repeatedly to accept any offer. It was only a mere half hour later that his phone rang, and it was Steward's lawyer's office setting up a date for the closing.

In a short two weeks, he would be living at the ocean with his family, praying on his next adventure. His heart fluttered with excitement at the thought. He really had no direction at all; he was ready though. So much of the country was changing right now; there was any number of directions he could choose to go, any type of business he might start. He had prayed for God's guidance and wisdom, but for now, he was looking forward to spending time with his family.

He and Chance left his office and walked the property. David watched the guests enjoying the different activities offered. Many of them were return guests David had come to know. Through word of mouth, new people were joining them regularly. Each of the cabins was full and booked ahead through Christmas and New Year's.

Lord, I pray the new owners keep this joy happening. Peace filled his heart in answer.

He wandered up to the barn and talked with Charlie, sharing the news, which felt bittersweet as he saw the sad look on his friend's face. He explained arrangements would be made for Duplin and Storm to be delivered to the Minnesott Beach property.

He went to see Duplin, and as he rubbed his forelock, he envisioned him galloping down the beach. "You'll see Marie soon," he mumbled to her beautiful white horse.

He'd decided to send the horses after the sale was final so he could be there when they were delivered. He knew Marie was looking forward to them coming and, considering Abigail was growing up quickly, decided a pony for her would make a good stable mate for the horses.

He went back to the inn and stood on the terrace while Chance wandered the tree line. He turned and leaned on the railing, remembering the first dance he'd awkwardly shared with Marie. She loved to dance. The memory inspired him, he knew what he wanted to do for her.

———⁓ᴍⱺⱺⱺ⟲ʁⱺⱺᴛⱺⱺⱺⱳ———

"What a fantastic idea," Marie said as she held her dress up in front of her, looking at herself in the mirror.

It was a long trip for Abigail, but David wanted the three of them to spend time as a family, one last time, at the inn. He had booked their favorite band and purchased beautiful dresses for his girls for their night of dancing.

She looked at her husband's reflection as he watched her. He looked happy. Marie felt blessed for having met and married such a thoughtful man. "Abigail, honey, come see."

Abigail had been running around the suite excitedly and came to her mom as soon as her name was called. Their relationship had changed a lot since Marie began to follow her husband's suggestions. She did feel more relaxed, and Abigail listened to her now, most of the time.

"Come see what Daddy got us." She put her dress down and picked up Abigail's. Kneeling before the mirror, she held it up to their daughter so she could see.

"Pretty," Abigail said.

Marie turned her head toward David. "Thank you."

Abigail ran out from behind the dress and hugged her father's legs. "Thank you, Daddy."

He bent down and hugged her little, pudgy frame. "You're welcome." Standing up, he picked her up in his arms. "Now I'm going downstairs to see how everything's coming along. I'll leave you two to get dressed and will see you soon." He brushed Abigail's nose with his finger and snuggled deep into her neck, giving her a quick kiss as she giggled.

Marie was looking forward to their being together again, but for tonight, she looked forward to spending time with those they had become close to. Her parents were joining them, and all the staff members who were not working were invited; those working were expected to come and enjoy some time at this good-bye party as well.

Good-bye—the words caught Marie, just a little. Change, of course, is hard, and good-bye seemed final. The inn itself had been so much a part of Marie. It had been the stage for her growing up, both physically and spiritually.

After David left, she quickly got changed.

"Mommy, you pretty," Abigail responded when Marie returned to the living room to get her dressed.

"Why, thank you, honey. Are you ready to put your dress on too?"

"Abigail pretty too?" she asked with brightness in her eyes.

"Of course." Marie picked her up and hugged her tightly. "Abigail's pretty too."

Marie felt like a queen as she entered the great room holding Abigail's hand. The dresses David had picked out were perfect. She felt her cheeks get hot as people turned around to look at them. Suddenly, the sound of applause began, which grew with every set of hands that joined. Marie stopped, dropped Abigail's hand, stepped away, and bowed toward her daughter. The applause for Abigail instantly grew thunderous.

David stepped through the crowd, clapping as he came. There was a smile on his face, but Marie could have sworn she saw the shine of tears in his eyes. He leaned in and kissed her cheek, offered his arm to Marie, and took the hand of his daughter. Together, they struck a beautiful picture of what family was meant to look like: love, pure and unconditional.

They danced to the music and conversed with those they would soon be leaving.

Marie had the most memorable night. She took David to the terrace for their final dance under the stars and whispered into his ear, "I want to thank you for all you've done for me. I love you."

CHAPTER

29

David had spent nearly three months in prayer for the next step of their life. Not feeling any direction from God yet, he enjoyed being home with his family. He had deposited the money from the sale of the inn in Wilson, at the Branch Banking and Trust Company and took sparingly from the account as they needed. As far as he could figure, there was more than enough money for them to live on and still invest when the time was right.

They had purchased a Shetland pony for Abigail and had walked with her many times on the beach and around the paddock to get her used to riding. She loved her new pet, and he seemed to be a good fit in the barn. Abigail had named him Charlie since that was a name she often heard at the barn in Roxboro. David liked it.

The move didn't fare well for Chance, though. It hadn't been long after that something seemed wrong. He wasn't eating much and wasn't nearly as active anymore. Given the time David had him he figured he'd be about fourteen, which was rather old for a dog. Maybe his life was tied to that old barn in Roxboro. After a couple weeks of this odd behavior, David found him curled up in the barn one morning.

"Chance, old boy, what's wrong?" David got down on one knee and stroked his head.

Outside of the lift of an eyebrow, Chance didn't offer any other sign of life. David sat down on the ground beside him and lifted his head, placing it gently on his lap. There he sat, patting him and talking quietly to him, until he passed away. David cried. Their connection had been special. It was going to feel strange not having him trot along behind him all the time.

He left Chance to tell Marie. They opted to not alarm Abigail, and when she was down for her afternoon nap, the pair held an emotional but brief service at the side of a hole David dug for him just past the pasture on the edge of the woods.

Later that day, they told Abigail, before she noticed him missing, that God called Chance home to be with him. Marie explained that they were putting a cross near the woods so they could have a place to think about him whenever they wanted.

Abigail seemed content with that information and wanted to carry the simple wooden cross David had nailed together. The three walked to the special place, and Abigail handed the cross to her dad so he could hammer it upright into the ground. After he was done, she held her hands up to be picked up by David, and then she wiped the tear from his cheek. She was a sweet girl, David thought as he held her tightly in his arms.

The next morning, the phone rang as they were getting ready to build sand castles together. David picked up the receiver. "Hello?"

"David, there's a problem. Have you heard?" The alarmed voice of Cameron Morrison was on the line.

"Cam, no, I haven't heard anything. Are you all right?" David was concerned for the strong emotion in his friend's voice. He sat down.

Marie held her hand up to David, assuring him to take his time, and she took Abigail out the door, leaving him to talk on the phone undisturbed.

"I don't know what's going to happen now, but the stock market just crashed. It's bad, David."

"You're kidding."

"I wish I was," Cameron answered.

"Don't get too worried. Let's just see what this means. Maybe it's just a fluke."

"Maybe, but panic's in the air."

"Keep me updated," David requested.

"Will do. I may just need you to come back to the capitol with some strong business ideas to help if things start heading downhill."

"Of course, let me know if you think I can help."

"I just hope your money's safe, David. A lot of it's gonna disappear, I'm afraid. What would that do to you and Marie?"

David had yet to absorb all that this historic event was going to mean. "Well, I'm not in debt, and my money is at the BB&T. Cam, it sounds like panic in your voice. Really, you need to step back and look at all this clearly."

"Clearly, our comforts, our lives are *clearly* going to change! David, think about what this might mean."

"Might, that's the key word here. Let's wait and see what's happening. Then we'll look at what can be done. Right now, you need to calm down just a bit." David kept his voice firm. He could sense the fear in his friend and prayed it wouldn't overwhelm him.

"I'll keep you posted." The line went dead.

David thought about what a crash in the stock market meant for him, their state, their neighbors, and their country. He rose and went to the radio, clicking it on, then sat back down and listened to the same hysteria he heard in Cam's voice.

He shook his head, feeling strongly that the fear voiced over these airwaves was going to create fear, a fear that didn't need to be multiplied to the degree he imagined it would. It was the same mentality he had used to make money in business. He clicked the radio off and headed out the door to see his wife and daughter.

"Daddy, how do you like it?" Abigail asked.

David smiled as his daughter called for his attention. That is what brings joy: purity and simplicity. God's peace could be found in these things, not in money. He walked down to the water's edge where the sand was cooler and turned back to look at the sand sculpture she and Marie were working on.

"Honey, that's a beautiful umbrella. You ladies have done a spectacular job," he answered

Abigail smiled. "Can you see the colors, Daddy? It's red, white, and blue, just like a flag."

Marie stood up and stretched her back, smiling. "You're cute, Abigail."

"Mommy thought it was white with red spots. She's silly," Abigail responded, looking at her father.

"You got a lot done. I do see the colors of the flag in it. It's very patriotic."

"Patrio…what's that?" Abigail asked.

"Patriotic, honey, it means that you believe in your country, you support it," David explained.

"I believe in God. Does that mean the same thing?" Abigail asked.

David and Marie both chuckled.

"That's a great start, Abigail," David responded. "I pray he's in the hearts of many Americans right now." David looked out over the ocean. "That's the only way we're going to make it through these tough times."

Marie came up beside him as he stood looking at the horizon. She wrapped her arm around his. "Honey, is everything okay?"

"I don't think so, Marie. We really need to trust in God and cling to him."

Marie and David sat together in the living room each night after Abigail was tucked in bed and listened to the horror experienced

in their country as it unfolded on the radio. They listened to stories of loss, fear, and even suicide.

"There must be some that aren't affected by this," Marie mused on the night following Black Tuesday.

"Certainly there are," David answered.

She sat up from the comfort of his side. "Who?" Marie asked.

"Us," he answered confidently.

"I guess that would also mean others of faith," she responded as she resumed her spot in the warmth given by her husband.

"I told Cameron I'd go to Raleigh if he needed me to. Outside of simply supporting him and our state, I don't know what good I'd be. I wouldn't run business the way many of these people have. To put your family in debt in the hope of getting rich just seems backward to me. It seems there was a lot of temptation involved, and these are the natural consequences."

David became quiet as the radio continued its droll reports of doom and forecasts of fear. He was thinking as he was listening. After a time, he came to a realization. "It almost seems as though this is what happened with the Gold Rush. So many people were chasing a dream of fortune that only a few had really found. I'm sure you learned about the people that flocked to join the Gold Rush, bringing their families along to experience disease, obsession, and death. Money's a temptation that leads you away from faith, away from trust."

Marie nodded. "Satan can be powerfully influential, can't he?"

"I'd say. We have a large amount of money in savings. I'm unsure of what'll become of it, but I don't feel led to join in any of this panic. It's wrong. If God intends for us to start over again, then we'll do it."

Marie hugged him tightly. "I'm glad to hear you say that, David. I trust him. He has a plan for us."

As time wore on and the Great Depression was felt all over the world, David and Marie were comfortable in their trust of God's will. It did not matter that the value of their home had plummeted, because they owned it. It did not matter that they had not invested their money, because it would have been lost if they had. As banks were closing all around them, they decided not to take their money out. If their large amount of savings could, in some way, help their bank stay afloat, then it would remain where it was.

David realized that selling the Foxglove Inn to Steward Enterprises actually helped not only the employees, but the Tate's, whom he did not sell to. It was clear now that they would not have survived the changes in the economy. David believed it was because Steward Enterprises had spread its value and debts over a large amount of properties that they were able to keep the inn open, saving the jobs of those that had invested their time and talents with David from its beginning, including Marie's father.

As time wore on and the fall-out was being realized, it was time to get busy working toward a positive future. David began making business trips to Raleigh to work with Cameron and the state officials in an attempt to steady the economy.

CHAPTER

30

A year and a half had passed since the stock market crash, and David had been working at the state capitol intensely for many months, travelling home for visits. He stepped onto the porch overlooking the ocean after searching through the house for his wife and daughter. He had been away for two weeks and was missing them terribly. Abigail was turning four soon, and though he was often gone for weeks at a time and missed her while away, he made sure their time together was meaningful. They were close.

He could see Marie sitting in a chair near the water's edge facing the ocean; the tide was coming in. Abigail was building an elaborate sculpture in the sand. The beach was a large canvas on which to create, and it was washed clean each day, encouraging a new design.

He headed down the stairs when Abigail caught sight of him.

"Daddy!" she shouted.

David waved to her and saw Marie turn in her chair to look. She waved. Abigail got up and ran toward him.

"Daddy!" she exclaimed again as she reached him. "Come see what I made." She held his hand and pulled to get him moving quicker.

"Okay, okay," David said, laughing, his heart filling with joy. Returning home always felt good. "I'm coming, dear." He picked up his pace.

"You'll have to guess, Daddy. See! What do you think it is?"

They arrived at the sight of her creation.

David scratched his chin, hopefully showing how deep in thought he knew she wanted him to be. "Hmm," he mused.

"Daddy, come on. Guess," Abigail insisted.

"I know, I know, give me a minute. I'm thinking."

Abigail turned to face the sculpture, which filled the space of five feet around but lay low to the ground. She cocked her head to the side and said, "It looks pretty clear to me. Daddy, what do you think it is?"

"Well, let's see. I think I see a hat, a great big sun hat." He saw her stiffen up. "Okay, that's not it. It's a chandelier, like the one in the house." She turned away, looking dismayed.

He felt a twinge of sadness and felt bad for teasing her. He reached down and embraced her shoulders from behind. "Honey, that's the finest octopus I've ever seen. You're an amazing artist."

Abigail spun around and smiled brightly at her father. "Do you really like it?"

"How could I not? It's fantastic!" He kissed her on the forehead. "I'm gonna go say hi to Mommy, honey. I love you."

"Okay, I love you too. I've got to finish quickly before the water comes and cleans it away." She dropped to her knees to complete the detailed marine-life sculpture she'd worked hard on all day.

David walked to his wife, who had been watching them from her seat, and bent down to kiss her. "Hi, honey, how are you?"

"I'm good. It's so beautiful here, you know." She turned to look out over the ocean again.

"I know it is. Are you enjoying it here?" David watched her. Concern touched his heart. She was different lately, though he wondered if it was because he was not home with her all the time.

"Oh yes, very much," she said.

"It looks like Abigail's had a great day," David said. They both turned to look at her.

"She's been working hard," Marie said. "You should've seen the sculpture she made yesterday."

"What was it?" David looked at his wife's face. She was beautiful.

"A turtle, a really big turtle, and the shell was elaborately decorated. She spent hours on it. It was hard to get her to come in for lunch."

David leaned forward and kissed his wife. "I love you."

"I love you too. I've missed you."

"I know. I've missed you too. I'm sorry I'm away so much. Is it hard on you?" he asked.

"Oh no, it's fine. I shouldn't have said that," Marie answered.

"What? That you missed me?" David chuckled as Marie smiled sheepishly. That was the woman he'd fallen in love with. "I want to know that you miss me, but I don't want you to be sad."

Marie looked up at David and into his eyes, which was something he hadn't been seeing much of lately. He was concerned that his work was affecting their marriage.

"I love you, David. That's why I miss you, because I love you. I'm proud of you, and really, I'm happy here. I feel blessed for what we have and where we live. Thank you for working hard and loving us. Don't worry." She reached up and caressed his face.

He felt emotion welling up within him; he had been worrying. Her behavior seemed to indicate she was falling away from him. It seemed like it had been nearly half a year or so that she'd been becoming more and more distant. When he had first noticed, it was subtle, but lately, she seemed distracted most of the time. It was moments of clarity such as this that reminded him of who he had fallen in love with. He felt the tears sting his eyes.

"Oh, David." Marie rose and wrapped her arms around him, compelling his tears to flow freely. "Don't cry. Are you okay?"

David wrapped his arms around Marie and held tightly, clinging to her. He was not just embracing his love; he was holding on with all his might to this moment, to this connection he had been missing. He prayed, reaching out for strength and pleading for life to remain as it was at this moment. He felt peace fill him deeply and knew that God was with them.

Lord, your will be done. I trust you. Please give me wisdom and understanding.

David felt that word that had followed him throughout his life. *David, I gave you compassion. This, I called you for.*

Chills ran down his spine, and he took a deep, slow breath before standing tall again and looked down at his wife. He rubbed her back. "I'm fine, honey. I've just missed you two so much."

"Come, let's go in and get some supper going."

They walked together, Marie embracing David's arm.

"Abigail, honey, we're heading indoors," Marie called as they passed her and her octopus.

"Okay, Mommy."

David winked at her as he caught her eye in passing. Inside, David settled onto a stool at the kitchen counter and visited with Marie as she pulled a chicken out of the refrigerator, prepared it, and tucked it into the oven. She cut up some potatoes to put on the stove for mashed potatoes.

"Honey, you're making my favorite meal?"

"I wanted you to enjoy your first night back at home." After covering them with water in the pot, she left them on the stove to turn on later and went to sit beside David at the counter. "How's work been?"

"It's been good, as good as can be expected under the circumstances. Since the crash, we've really been scrambling to come up with ways to regain the confidence of our country. It's tough for everyone right now, though."

"I can only imagine. It's been amazing listening to the news lately. Do you think we could still lose everything like so many others?"

"God's protected us. We own our home, and our bank's still open. I thought I was waiting to invest that money in another business, but maybe I was meant to just keep it in the bank.

Maybe it has helped keep it afloat. I can't tell you how thankful I am for my relationship with Christ right now. Not that money's important, but we're stable, and I'm hopeful I can help others. I pray the Lord gives me direction on how."

"I'm so proud of who you are, David," Marie said. "You're a man of such compassion."

There was that word again; chills passed through him as the word left his wife's lips: compassion. He knew it was God confirming to him the path he was on.

Lord, if all you allowed in my young life was to create a compassion in me that would help others, then I'm thankful for all I went through.

The screen door opened, and David turned to watch his little girl come wandering in. She was humming to herself.

"Hi, sweetie, did you finish your octopus?"

"Yup, it's all done, Daddy. Do you wanna see it now?"

Marie had gotten up, gone to the sink, and gotten a cup of water. "Here, honey."

Abigail went to her mother's side and took the cup, drinking long and deep while looking at her dad over the top.

"Sure."

He joined them at the sink, leaning over the head of his sweet angel to kiss his wife.

CHAPTER

31

This time David's visit home was markedly different. He watched his wife become concerned over things that didn't seem real, at least not to him. By the time his stay was coming to an end, he found himself worrying about leaving.

"Marie, do you know where my newest pair of jeans went? I was going to pack them," David hollered from the bedroom door. He had his half filled suitcase open on the bed.

Marie came rushing up the stairs and looked scared when she came into the room.

"Marie, honey, what's wrong? Are you okay?" David turned his full attention to his wife, holding her by the arms and looking into her face.

"What did you say was missing?" she asked.

"My new jeans," David answered. "It's not a big deal, though."

Marie broke from David's hold and briskly walked the length of the room, looking suspiciously around. She went to the window and looked outside, fingering the lock.

"Honey, what's wrong?" he asked, very concerned.

"I thought I heard something a couple of days ago," she whispered. "A couple of men were talking quietly, but when I looked around, I couldn't find them. I think they snuck in here."

David took her words and behavior in but couldn't believe how irrational she seemed. "Honey, I'm sure nobody snuck in our house."

Marie turned around abruptly to face him. "Your pants are missing, and I heard someone in here. It makes sense to me."

David's mind was racing. He couldn't get a grip on what he was witnessing, let alone know what to do about it. He walked up to Marie and reached for her. She braced as if unsure whether to allow his touch, but then let him hold her hands.

"Marie, honey, I'm sure nobody came in here."

She pulled away and walked around him. "You don't have to believe me, but I know someone was here."

She left the room. He heard her go back down the stairs. David looked at the rocks and the ocean beyond through the window and shook his head. *Lord, what's going on? What's wrong with her? She's becoming someone I don't recognize. I'm worried, and I don't know what to do. Is it because I'm gone so much? Please help me.* He walked back to his suitcase and sat down beside it. *Help me know what to do, Father.*

Slowly, feeling quite unsettled about it, David finished packing before going to put Abigail to bed.

He found his daughter curled up on the couch on the porch with a book open in her lap. He settled in beside her, and she glanced up.

"Hi, Daddy, can I read to you?"

"Sure, honey. I'd love to hear a story," David responded without really paying attention.

Abigail had learned her alphabet and knew some words by sight, but her reading was made up. She ran her fingers under the words as her mother had taught her, but her eyes were on the pictures. David was listening to her active imagination expressed in the adventures Princess Abby was experiencing.

The door opened, and Marie stepped halfway through it, peering left down the beach, then right to the rocky shore as if she were looking for someone. Abigail continued with her story, unaffected by her mother's presence. The door closed as Marie went back inside.

"Daddy, don't you think Princess Abby's beautiful?" Abigail asked.

"Yes, honey. She is," David answered, though he wasn't really paying attention.

"See." Abigail said as she pointed to the picture of a girl riding her tricycle on a sidewalk. "Princess Abby's horse is bringing her into the woods. She's scared."

Abigail continued reading to David about the scary woods and the wild animals when Marie came walking around the side of the house, still appearing as though she were looking for someone.

"I'll be right back, honey," David whispered to Abigail as he got up.

He went to the railing to watch Marie, who had now walked out onto the beach and stood looking toward the boat docks in the distance. After some time, she turned back toward the house and looked up at David. He waved timidly to her. She looked away as if irritated. David returned to Abigail and stood in front of her.

"Hey, Abigail, it's time to brush your teeth and go to bed now."

She uncurled her legs from beneath her as she answered, "Okay, Daddy."

She stood up on the couch, and he turned around, prompting her to climb on his back.

"Giddy up, Daddy!"

David opened the door and trotted to the stairwell, which led up to a second bathroom and two bedrooms. Abigail dismounted on her bed, and David left while she changed into her pajamas, meeting her minutes later in the bathroom. Abigail stepped up onto the stool so she could reach the sink.

"Okay, here." David had put a small amount of toothpaste on her toothbrush and handed it to her. He sang the ABCs while she brushed. She always spat when he reached Z. It was a ritual she enjoyed.

David bent down with his back to her once more. "Okay, climb on."

Abigail jumped on. He trotted out the door and back into her bedroom, where he dropped her onto her bed. She was giggling as she pulled back her covers and crawled under.

"Daddy, are you leaving again?"

"Yes, honey, early in the morning. I'll call you, though," he answered.

"Can I read to you on the telephone?" she asked.

"Of course you can. I love to hear about Princess Abby's adventures." David watched Abigail yawn, and he tousled her hair. "Sweet dreams, honey."

Abigail sat up straighter and reached out to hug her dad, who smiled as he leaned down to embrace his little girl.

"Sweet dreams to you too, Daddy," she said.

Letting go, she wiggled down under her covers. David kissed her forehead, clicked off the lamp, and walked to the door, where he turned back to face her. "I love you, Abigail."

"I love you too, Daddy," she sleepily responded then rolled away from him.

He closed her door almost completely, leaving it open a crack before heading downstairs to try to resolve the division he was now feeling between he and Marie. She was sitting on the couch in the living room and tensed up visibly when he entered the room.

He walked up to face her. "Marie." David calmly prodded for her attention before sitting on the opposite side of the couch. "Marie, are you okay?"

"I'm fine." Her response sounded defensive.

"You seem angry with me. I don't like this separateness between us."

"You looked at me earlier like there was something wrong with me! I don't like that feeling! I thought someone was in our home, and you didn't seem concerned for us at all. Worse than that, it's clear you didn't even believe me. I know what I heard."

David took a breath, seeking a moment of sanity in the midst of this chaos. "Honey, I'm worried about you. You're acting"—he paused, thinking how best to say what he was feeling—"different lately. Are you afraid of being here alone while I'm away?"

"Acting differently?" Marie became tense once more. "I'm not afraid." Marie hunched her shoulders as if defeated. "I love being here."

"But you thought someone had come in. I know that frightened you."

Marie seemed to consider her words carefully before she spoke next. "I thought someone stole from us. Certainly I'd be angry if that had happened. You worked hard for the things we have." Marie began to fidget a bit.

"Honey, what is it?" David asked, hating the awkwardness of their conversation. At times like this it was clear something was wrong, she was so childlike. But at other times she seemed rational. It made him wish they could go back in time, back before they moved. Perhaps it was simply the move and his being away that was causing her odd behavior.

Marie started crying. "I found your jeans. They'd fallen onto the floor near the washer."

David slid a little closer to his wife and rubbed her back. She continued crying softly.

"It's okay, Marie. Hey, why don't you tell me what you've been feeling, what you've been experiencing? I want to understand. I love you. Please tell me."

David turned Marie to face him as he would a small child. He wanted her to look at him, though, to see how strong his support of her was.

"Please don't be afraid to talk to me about what you're going through. There's nothing you can do or say that will change my love of you. You're a gift from God, a gift I'm blessed to have."

He looked at her, hoping his words were the encouragement she needed to trust him before he prodded further, but she didn't seem to be listening.

"Why are you behaving differently? What's happening?"

"I don't know what's wrong. They told me about it, but I wasn't sure."

"What do you mean?" She wasn't making any sense, and David was really confused now. "Who?" he asked.

"I don't know, but they said it. I feel like that's what they talked about. It's the war that killed him that's bothering me. Or maybe that's why they said it."

David reached up to put a strand of her hair behind her ear that had fallen in front of her face. "I'm not sure I understand, honey. Do you think this is happening because you're alone here without me?" David was grasping at logic. Marie's words had none. He realized that his attempts to understand weren't making sense either.

"I don't know. I don't know. I'm confused. I was so sure there was someone here. I could hear someone, but when I looked I couldn't see them."

"Did you hear them today? Is that why you were looking down the beach?"

"There was someone. They were talking about the war and the fighting. They were on the docks. I could hear them," she answered.

David held his thoughts to himself; this was entirely impossible. Something was tragically wrong, and he didn't know what to do.

CHAPTER

32

It was an early August Monday morning in 1931 when David arrived at work in Raleigh, feeling wrong about leaving his wife and daughter behind at their home on the ocean, hours away. He determined he would work four long days and head home Thursday night. He was planning to meet with Cam to brainstorm ideas for the state project they were scheduled to present to the legislature soon. It had been almost two years since the stock market crash, and they were determined to turn things around.

Cameron Morrison often referred to David as "The man who could build success out of thin air." David knew his successes were not his own doing. He believed that if God had a plan, it simply would be. He certainly didn't want to start something without God dictating. It was an amazing feeling to be part of something bigger than oneself.

There was a firm knock on his office door. "Come in, it's open!" David hollered.

The stately figure of Cameron Morrison passed confidently through. "David, how are you?" He stepped up to David's desk, holding out his hand.

"Cam." David rose and shook the hand extended to him. "I'm well. How are you today?"

"Good, thanks," he answered.

"Have a seat," David offered as he came around his desk and sat opposite his friend. "I've been busy and haven't really gotten much pulled together for our meeting, I'm sorry."

"Not a problem. Where do you want to go for lunch today? Are you craving anything in particular?" Cam asked.

His suggestion of lunch surprised David. He was thinking so much of his wife that he hadn't realized he was hungry. "Not really. If you don't mind I'd rather you decide."

"Sounds good to me. I've got pasta on my mind. Let's walk down to the Italian Eatery on the corner." Cam stood up, ready to go.

David smiled as he rose to follow. His friend loved food.

The walk to the restaurant was quiet, and once the orders were placed, Cam spoke. "David, what's wrong? You seem distracted."

David pushed himself from the table and leaned back in his chair. "I'm not sure how to answer that." He took a breath and looked at his friend. "I think something's wrong with my wife."

"Marie?" Cam sounded concerned. "What do you mean, you think something's wrong?"

"She's been acting strangely for a while now, but this last weekend—" David hesitated as he considered what to say. He felt comfortable with Cam, but he wasn't quite sure what ramifications might be experienced by sharing the condition he felt his wife was really in.

"David, what happened?"

"I don't know really." How do you explain that your wife might be crazy, especially to a politician with whom you have worked closely with for years? The social fallout concerned him. "Forget it, Cam. I don't really know what to say."

Cam leaned forward, propping his elbows on the table. "David, we've been friends a long time. I hope you feel comfortable confiding in me. It's clear that something's wrong."

"Cam," David watched his face to measure any reaction as he continued, "I'm afraid my wife is mentally ill."

Cam did lean in a little deeper, but the look David saw in his eyes was concern, not fear as he had expected.

"I don't know. Just when I decide she is, she acts normal again. Maybe it's because I'm away from home so much. We were together every day at the inn. Maybe she's just lonely."

"Can you describe her behavior to me, David? Help me understand."

David thought for a few minutes. "At first, I just thought she was lonely. I know she's got Abigail, but I'm sure that's not the same as regular adult conversation. She'd talk to herself."

"I think we all do that, don't we?" Cam asked.

"That was my initial reaction, but she really seems to be talking a lot, as if to someone."

Cam sat back and chuckled lightly. "Does anyone answer?"

David's look firmed in discouragement.

"I'm sorry, David," Cam offered. "I can see you're really concerned."

Even though he was sure he'd made a big social mistake stepping into this conversation, David figured he had nothing more to lose, at this point. "That's what concerned me. She was not only talking to herself, there were many times it sounded like she was answering someone, as if there really was someone asking her questions."

"Really?" Cam asked, seeming much more interested now. "Are you serious?"

David nodded. "At first, I figured I was thinking into it, but it's become really obvious."

"Have you asked her about it?"

"I did this weekend. She got really upset. I don't know what to do, but I'm at the point that I don't feel comfortable leaving them home alone."

The men became quiet as the waitress came with their lunches. They ate in silence as David turned his thoughts heavenward. *Lord, please give me wisdom and protect us. I can only imagine what exposing this means for us now. I pray I did the right thing in talking to Cam.*

He felt badly for talking about his wife behind her back. She was his closest confidante, his wife, his lover, and his best friend. It felt wrong to talk about her to someone else. That heaviness left him feeling evil, in some way.

Cam picked up the check when it came. "I'll take this, David. You've got a lot going on right now."

David took a breath to protest, but then let it out in acceptance. "Thanks, Cam."

They got up from the table, left the restaurant, and walked in silence.

As they reached the steps of the building David was staying in to work, he turned toward his friend. "I'm sorry, Cam. I feel like I've wasted your time today. I can't focus on work right now. Can we reschedule?"

Cam reached out and shook David's hand but didn't let go; his grip was firm as he reached up to grasp David's shoulder with his free hand. "I understand. Call me when you get a chance. I'm really sorry for what you and Marie are going through. If there's anything I can do to help, please let me know."

David smiled weakly in response. "Thanks, Cam. I don't even know what I can do. I'm praying for direction."

When David reached his office, the phone was ringing. He chose not to answer it. He was emotionally drained and needed quiet time. No sooner did he sit down at his desk and drop his head to his hands than it started ringing again. *Lord, no. I can't talk to anyone right now,* he prayed, but it continued, beckoning him to answer.

"Hello?"

"They're coming back." Marie's voice was frantic as she shouted over the phone. Then suddenly, she whispered, "David, they're coming."

David's senses were instantly heightened. "Who, Marie? Who are you talking about? Who's coming?"

"I've got to get Abigail out of here. They said they're going to hurt her."

"Marie, honey, I don't understand. Who's going to hurt her?" Her panic was transferring its energy to him now.

She wasn't listening to him, he could tell. "Where should we go? David, where should we go? Should we take the horses and hide in the woods? They know my car, so I can't take that."

David didn't know what to say or really what to do. His wife's sanity was completely gone, and she was bringing their daughter into it. *Dear Lord, give me wisdom.* He didn't know what Marie was going to do next. He couldn't reach the house in less than three hours on a good day.

He remembered how angry and defensive Marie became when he questioned her story, only a day earlier. If he questioned her now, there would be no telling what she would do, and Abigail might really be in danger. The thought crossed his mind to act as if she were not crazy, to go along with the situation as presented.

CHAPTER

33

"David, David, hurry! Where can we hide?" Marie sounded like she was about to give up on her husband's help.

Feeling almost uncomfortable joining the charade but trusting God's lead, he asked, "Marie, how long do you think you have?"

"One of them said he had to get the room ready for her. David, I'm scared. I don't want them to hurt her." Though her words expressed her concern, the intensity of her voice had subsided a bit.

"Listen to me carefully. Lock the doors, close the windows, and take Abigail to the closet under the stairs. I'm going to call Pastor Steve and have him go to the house and stay with you until I get home. He's not far from you."

"No, David, they're evil. They'll find us. We have to leave!" Desperation was escalating again in Marie's voice.

"Honey, listen. Do what I'm telling you." David tried to keep his voice calm for her, but he was feeling more and more anxious to get off the phone and head home.

"How will I know it's him, then?" Marie asked. "They're sneaky. They could look like him."

David was searching through his address book for the phone number of the pastor while trying to coach his wife on what to do. "I'll tell him to knock three times. You'll know the code. Three knocks, Marie."

"Three knocks," she repeated. "But what if they know the code?"

"Marie, trust me," David demanded. "Lock up and hide. I'm on my way. I'll see you soon."

"Okay," Marie responded as though she wasn't really listening anymore.

David hung up the phone and picked the receiver up once more, dialing the number of Pastor Steve, praying he would be there. His heart was pounding. For a moment, he felt fear grip his heart as he realized their secret was about to be exposed in dramatic fashion. After a couple rings, he heard the familiar, soothing voice of the pastor of their church.

"Hello?"

"Pastor, this is David Towell."

"Hi, David, how are you?" he asked.

"We're having a crisis right now, and I was hoping you were available to help."

"Of course," the pastor answered. "What's the problem?"

"Marie's at home with Abigail, but she's having a breakdown or something. I'm in Raleigh. I can't get to her quickly."

"I can head over there right away," Pastor Steve offered.

"Thanks. There's a catch though. You have to knock three times."

"Three times?" David could hear the confusion in his voice.

"She thinks there are people coming to hurt Abigail. I told her to lock the house and hide and that you'd knock three times so she'd know it was you. I know it sounds crazy, but I didn't know what else to suggest. She's been acting very different lately," David explained the best he could in few words. "I'll meet you there as soon as I can."

"Oh, David, I'm sorry. I'll head over there right now."

Pastor Steve was always so peaceful. David thought highly of him. Though it was difficult to expose the truth of their situation, he knew he could trust their spiritual leader to help. "Thank you, pastor. I'll see you shortly."

David stepped out of his office and got in the elevator. He was thankful it was empty. He needed time, brief as it would be, to seek God's peace. *Oh, please help us, Lord. Guide me. Protect my family.*

He leaned against the wall and felt peace touch his soul. When the doors opened, he took a deep breath and stepped out.

———·❧·———

Something had gone wrong, terribly wrong. He could see the lights of the police car and ambulance before he reached the house. He sped up and closed the final distance in seconds. Once he slammed the car into park and got out, he raced up the stairs and through the door that was standing open. A quick glance at the doorway showed the door had been broken into.

"Daddy!" David heard the sweet sound of his little girl, who ran to him. He reached down, and she jumped into his arms. Bewildered, he glanced around.

Officer Hall approached him. "Mr. Towell, I'm afraid we've had some trouble with your wife."

David kept looking around, trying to figure out what happened. "What do you mean? Where is she? Where's Pastor Steve?"

"I was keeping your daughter company." He winked at Abigail in David's hands. She snuggled deeper into her father's embrace.

"Where's my wife, officer?" Every hair on his head was standing on end.

"She's upstairs with the pastor and the medic."

David put Abigail down. "Are you okay?"

She nodded in response.

"Stay here, honey." He kissed her absentmindedly on top of her head then turned to rush up to their room.

Pastor Steve met him at the top of the stairs. "David, Marie's not well."

"What happened?" David tried to look around the pastor into their bedroom. The door had been closed partially, hiding his view. "I want to see her."

"That's not a good idea." He stepped forward to block David's passage. "Let me explain. When I got here I knocked, just like you told me, three times. I waited a few minutes, and she didn't answer. I tried the handle and called out to her, but she still didn't answer, so I went around to the back porch and tried that door. It was locked too. I peered in the window, and just as I leaned in to look past the glare of the sun, the window shattered."

"Oh my God, it was Marie." David's heart sank. The magnitude of their situation was growing. He felt compelled to get to her, but Pastor Steve held him back.

When David stepped back once more, the pastor resumed his story. "She tried to hit me through the window with a hammer, and her arm caught on the broken glass. She was screaming at me to stay away from Abigail. I tried to talk to her through the broken window, but she kept threatening me. I could see she was bleeding very badly, and though I told her she was hurt, she wouldn't listen. She was telling me I was using the pastor's body to trick her."

David listened, shaking his head in disbelief.

The pastor continued, "I'm sorry, David, but I had to leave to get help. She wouldn't let me in, and she acted like I was going to hurt them. I drove back to town and went to the police station for help. Officer Hall radioed for the ambulance."

David looked up tearfully and asked, "Marie? Is she okay?"

"She's sedated. They're tending to her cuts before putting her in the ambulance. She needs psychiatric care, David."

David's heart dropped. He had watched her illness grow over time; he knew she needed help, but mental patients were put away and forgotten. He couldn't imagine what they were going to do to her.

"How was Abigail when you got in?" David asked.

"They had to break the door in. Marie wouldn't listen to us. She was a different person. David, she certainly wasn't the Marie I know."

David was nodding his head in agreement. "I know."

"Once we got in, she tried to attack us with the hammer again. She kept saying we couldn't have her daughter. She ran upstairs, and Officer Hall was able to catch her and hold her while the medic gave her a shot to calm her. I didn't look for Abigail until they got her under control."

David looked past him, imagining what his wife had just gone through, the extreme fear she must have been experiencing. He was sure she believed "those people" had really come for Abigail.

Pastor Steve continued, "I called Abigail's name as I walked around the house. I was afraid Marie had done something with her. Finally, I heard her. She was crying. I opened the closet door under the stairs, and she was there. She looked so afraid. I stayed with her and tried to reassure her that she was fine, her mommy was fine, and you were on your way home. Officer Hall came downstairs a little while ago, and I asked her if she didn't mind if I went to see her mommy."

"Pastor, I don't know what to do. Lord"—David looked skyward—"why is this happening to us?"

CHAPTER

34

Abigail had gone home with Pastor Steve. David followed the ambulance to the hospital in New Bern. He was filled with anxiety the whole ride there. He could imagine how uncomfortable his daughter was feeling right now being away from home, especially after such a frightening experience.

He tried to talk to Marie as they were bringing her out of the house to the ambulance, but she didn't seem to notice him. She wasn't making any sense. Due to the sedative, her words were barely audible, but she continued to mumble about "them." It was ironic that her imaginary fears became reality, like a self-fulfilling prophecy. "They" were coming to do something bad, and ultimately, "they" came, and it did turn out bad.

What was this going to mean to their family? How could he take care of Abigail if something were really wrong with Marie? How could he care for Marie if there was something really wrong with her? If he was unable to stop this horrible event from happening, how on earth could he make things normal going forward for all of them?

Suddenly, David felt alone and overwhelmed. His whole future, their whole future, had taken an unexpected turn into something very dark. He drove, staring at the lights of the ambulance as they turned in circles before him, mesmerizing him.

He thought of the secret that grew out of control too fast. He thought of the image people had of him that would surely change. He was concerned that, after all the help he had been giving, now he would be shunned. How could he be of assistance? He feared people would not be able to see beyond the failed mental health of his wife.

As the ambulance pulled into the drive of the hospital and rain started falling through the darkness, he reached his end and turned his thoughts heavenward in shame. "Oh dear God, my Father! Forgive me for my thinking."

Once the car was placed in park, David broke down and sobbed. "This is not my life, but yours. My wife's future is in your hands, not mine." He shuddered and took a deep breath. "And our daughter is your child, not ours. How have I forgotten you in these few months of being busy? I've grown arrogant as I've focused on helping others."

After a moment of quiet soul searching, David envisioned himself kneeling at Jesus' feet. "Lord, please forgive me." His head was bowed as his mind cleared, and for a moment, he was not sitting in the rain while his wife was being treated like a mental patient, he was peacefully held in Jesus's embrace, feeling his unconditional love—that powerful and healing unconditional love.

I forgive you, David. I gave my life for you long ago. Be comforted. My helper, the Holy Spirit, is with you to guide you. Trust me.

David raised his head and watched in his rearview mirror as they unloaded his wife from the ambulance and went through the hospital doors. He knew it was not time for him to enter that fray, not yet. This time was holy. He sobbed deeply, feeling the sadness and burden from deep within surface and reach God's light. There was freedom in this moment, a freedom he wanted to be sure to absorb.

He bowed his head. "Thank you, Lord. I do trust you and will be there for my family as you dictate. Unconditional love, compassion—these are words you've impressed on me frequently throughout our walk together. I want to offer these and let my loved ones be who you want, not who I wish they would be. I pray for your strength in my weakness and that I forever rely on you. In Jesus' name, amen."

Taking a deep breath, David opened the car door and entered the downpour that drenched him before he even reached the emergency room door. Once he got under cover, he shook his head to get the rain off and couldn't help the smile that curved his lips, momentarily.

"Thanks, Lord, for the cleansing. You knew I needed that."

David hired a nanny to stay at the house with Abigail, affording him the freedom to be at the hospital whenever Marie needed him. Abigail seemed none the worse for wear, even though her mommy was not home. David told her he would take her to visit soon. She seemed content with that news, though he was unsure when that might be possible. Abigail easily accepted whatever God allowed, which was refreshing to David. That was a picture of the faith he desired, the faith of a child.

David split his time between home and the hospital in the days following Marie's admittance. Marie was sedated and shackled, and David was unable to talk with her. The doctor explained that each time they brought her out of sedation, she became very agitated. In their opinion, she was hallucinating and could act on voices she was hearing. They determined she was a danger to herself and others.

After evaluating Marie's behavior in the hospital, interviewing David, the officer, the minister, and the medic that went to their house the night Marie was hurt, the staff psychologist diagnosed her with a mental illness called schizophrenia—a horrible condition for which there was no hope.

David tried to explain that Marie was a person, a mother, and wife, but they didn't seem to want to hear that. They explained that she was sick and dangerous. They were trying to impress on David that not only did his wife become injured due to this illness, but his daughter could have become hurt, or worse, if he hadn't called for help.

Though he assured them he could stay home and care for her, they insisted she needed to remain hospitalized, and in fact, it had become widely believed in the mental health field that people with this disorder should separate from friends and family. Those personal ties were now thought to contribute to the symptoms of the illness. David was no longer welcome to visit her.

His opinion or hopes certainly didn't matter to them. He felt that in their eyes she was simply another mental patient. He sat at her bedside to say good-bye. She was bound down at her wrists and ankles and mumbling with her eyes closed. He was being watched by the nurses. She looked terrible. He wiped the drool that was escaping from the side of her dry lips, swallowed back his tears, and kissed her forehead. He prayed over her and offered her care up to his Lord and Savior.

Please help Marie, and help me let go of control, Father. It's obvious I have none anyway. Why do I struggle so?

Compassion, he heard in response.

He leaned in and slowly kissed her again, wishing, like some fairytale, his kiss would cause her to awaken and return to him whole. A tear slipped down his cheek and dropped on the pillow beside her. He touched it then brushed her cheek with his thumb. With the feeling of defeat slowly being replaced with the surety of faith, he turned and departed the New Bern Hospital to return home.

David knew the shallowness of the political atmosphere in Raleigh well. He'd recently been a part of it. He thought back over those days while driving home. He felt sure his time spent trying to reinvigorate the economy had come to an end. He was positive the gossip of his wife's sudden admission to a hospital replaced any interest in his aid. He hadn't bothered getting in touch with Cam since their ineffective lunch date almost a week earlier and was now accepting God had a plan in this too. He needed to return home to be with his child.

The fall chill was felt in the late night air as David made his way back home. *Dear Lord, please help me know what to do. If these professionals know what's best for my wife, then help me let go. I can't help but feel this isn't right. I don't want to fight for change if you're not dictating it, though. Please lay the path before me.*

David arrived home and climbed the stairs, dreading another night without his wife by his side. He missed her very much. He detoured at the top of the stairs and went to Abigail's door, pushing it open. Light from the hallway fell across her face, and he felt emotion well up inside. He fought the tears back, closed her door gently, and went back downstairs to sit on the porch.

He watched as the moonlight played on the ocean water and listened as the waves moved in gentle rhythm. He looked up at the stars and thought back to the sand sculptures they'd made together. He was startled when the door opened.

"Oh, you scared me, Dorothy."

"I'm sorry, Mr. Towell. I heard you come in and wanted to tell you Mr. Morrison was trying to reach you. He said to let you know he'll call again tomorrow. I told him I didn't know if you'd be home."

"Thank you." David turned back to face the ocean, unable to add another worry to the amount he already was struggling with. "How's Abigail?"

"Oh, yes, she's doing good, Mr. Towell, real good." Dorothy was a short, unassuming girl with dark brown hair, which was always tied back. She had a plump shape and a quiet voice. She was very young but reliable, and she was happy to assume the full responsibility of caring for a four-year-old girl. At seventeen, she was the oldest of seven children and understood all that needed to be done for both Abigail and the house. David knew she was a blessing.

"Thank you, Dorothy. I'll see you tomorrow, then," David said dismissively.

He had some explaining to do to Cam but dreaded hearing his life was the center of conversations around the state house. What his family was going through was nobody's business. It was difficult enough for him without the addition of public opinion. He rose from his seat and went to bed.

CHAPTER

35

David woke to the wonderful sound of his daughter calling his name. It brought a smile to his lips, which he swore he hadn't felt since Marie entered the hospital. She climbed up onto his bed and hugged him tightly.

"Your hug is just what I needed this morning. How did you know?"

"That's what God told me, Daddy," she answered.

David smiled and didn't doubt it.

"Are you coming down for breakfast?" she asked.

"Of course I am. Let me get dressed, and I'll be right down, okay?"

Abigail scurried off his bed. "I'll see you there," she said before closing the door behind herself.

As David was buttoning his shirt, he heard the phone ring, followed by Dorothy's footsteps to the bottom of the stairs. He reached for the door handle as he heard her call his name.

"I'm coming, Dorothy."

"Okay, Mr. Towell. It's Mr. Morrison for you."

"Thank you." David walked determinedly down the stairs, went to the phone receiver, which was laid down on the desk, and picked it up. "Hello?"

"David, it's nice to hear your voice! How's Marie doing?"

"Not very good, Cam." David didn't want to be having this conversation, and he chose not to hide that sentiment.

"I'm planning to come your way today. Are you going to be home?"

"I'm not up for it, Cam. I haven't spent any good time with Abigail in a while. I'd rather not have company."

"David, I'm worried about you. I can only imagine what you're going through. I'm going to stop by. I want to help you."

"Cam, I've been through hell, but that's nowhere near the trip my wife's been on. I don't believe I'd be any company right now."

"I understand, David, but I really think I should be with you. You're my friend. You were there for me when I lost my wife. I won't accept your refusal. I'll see you in a few hours." Cameron hung up.

David felt irritated, but as the voice of his daughter reached his ears, he smiled. *Lord, I let go. You can have it. May your will be done.*

He joined his daughter and Dorothy for breakfast. The pancakes she made were fabulous. At that moment, David realized that, though he'd eaten, he hadn't tasted food in a while. This was a testimony to letting go. He knew his wife would not be enjoying a sit-down breakfast with her family, but thoughts of this nature, David determined, were no longer going to undermine his trust in God for their lives.

"Abigail, what do you say we work on a sculpture today?"

"Really, Daddy? Do you have time?" she asked.

"I do," he responded.

"Are you going to see Mommy today?"

"No, honey, I'm staying home with you."

"I think she'll miss you," Abigail offered.

David looked at the concern on his little girl's face and ruffled her hair, offering a smile of comfort. "The doctors want to spend some time alone with her. They're trying to get just the right kind of help for her. They don't need Daddy hanging around watching them."

"Oh. Did you tell her I love her?" she asked.

"I sure did, and I know she could feel the love you sent her. Thank you for being such a sweet little girl. I know it's been really hard for you, not having Mommy here."

"She's coming home soon, isn't she?" she asked.

"I'm really not sure."

"But, Daddy, I love her. I want to see her."

"I do too." David took his daughter's hand in his and looked at her, feeling it was time to redirect their focus. "What shall we build?"

Abigail looked excited. "I've been thinking about building the castle from my book."

"A sandcastle?" David asked.

They both looked at each other and laughed. The normalcy of the suggestion wasn't lost on either of them.

"I don't know if we've ever built a good old-fashioned sandcastle. I think that'd be a challenge I'm up for."

They finished their breakfast and brought their empty plates to the sink where Dorothy was already working on cleaning up.

"Thank you, Dorothy. Breakfast was fabulous," David said before the pair headed out the door, hand in hand. He could feel his mood becoming increasingly lighter.

Abigail dropped David's hand and ran to get their buckets, shovels, and sticks, the tools of their craft. He walked down the steps toward the beach, where he paused to look over the grassy dunes separating their beach from the rocky shore. He and Marie had often cuddled in bed at night, listening to the water lapping the rocks their bedroom window overlooked. This house had been a wonderful escape for them, a time to really enjoy being family and a place to make memories he now imagined would hold him for the rest of his life.

As the pair was about to begin their work, David asked Abigail to get her book so he could copy the picture of the castle. When she returned, he realized it wasn't that easy; the castle was from her story, the one she'd made up. She offered to "read" it to him so he could imagine it better, which made him laugh.

After they had finished their creation, mostly Abigail's creation, they rode Charlie and Storm slowly down the beach.

"Daddy, we're gonna have to take Duplin out for rides for Mommy. He needs his exercise too."

"Good point, Abigail. I'll take turns with him."

"Okay."

The sweet nature of Abigail reminded David of Marie. They were so much alike. He watched her and felt proud of the kind person she was becoming when a sudden stab of fear broke his mood. Had he heard the word hereditary? Life had been such a blur. He had been interviewed about Marie's behavior leading up to her breakdown. It was coming back to him, little by little, but now, he was sure they'd mentioned schizophrenia was hereditary.

As they followed the beach for a while, David suggested they turn back to get some lunch. He waited for Abigail to turn Charlie around and reached out to slap her hand as she passed. She smiled, and he turned to follow, then trotted up alongside her.

They continued on in silence as David thought about Clara's mother. For years, Clara had taken care of her mother because she was unable to take care of herself. Scott had commented that she was crazy. David sat taller in his saddle, wondering if he had stumbled onto the link. Then he looked over at his little girl, who largely lived in an imaginary world. They thought it was because she needed a sibling or a friend, but she seemed content.

David had only told part of what was going on with Marie to her parents. He couldn't cope yet himself with the notion of her insanity. He explained she had to spend time in the hospital for nerve damage she suffered when she fell, accidentally putting her arm through a window. They offered to come stay with Abigail, but David knew they couldn't afford the trip or the time away from work, given the financial unrest the state was in. He now realized he needed to have an honest and very important conversation with them.

When David and Abigail returned home, Cameron Morrison was waiting for them. David sent Abigail in to help Dorothy while he took Charlie and Storm to the barn, Cam followed.

"David, I can only imagine what you're going through and the stress you're in. I thought I might be of some help."

"Cam, as I said, I'd rather not have company right now." David took the saddle and reigns off Storm and put them away then tended to Charlie. He brushed them down, filled their water, and threw some hay in their stalls before turning back to Cam. "My wife's in a hospital, and I'm not even welcome to be part of her life. Can you imagine that?" David could feel his temper rising. They walked back to the house where he sat down on the steps and took a deep breath, staring at the water in the distance but not really seeing it.

"I can help you, David," Cam said.

"I don't think so. I'm struggling enough right now trying to trust God's will."

"David, I know you weren't asking for my help, but I already called the State Hospital of Raleigh to secure a bed for Marie."

David looked at Cam, unsure if he should be furious or not. "I don't understand."

"I've made arrangements for her to be moved out of the New Bern facility as soon as you call them, authorizing the transfer to take place."

Cam had a lot of information, helpful and relevant. There was much they discussed, and as the conversation continued, David realized how much God had been preparing the way all along.

CHAPTER

36

Banks were failing, and jobs were in short supply. The Great Depression was gripping the country and starting to spread its ugly fingers worldwide. David's world was changing shape just as drastically but for different reasons. It was Christmas Eve, and though there was not much that money could buy to replace what David and Abigail were missing, they were able to bring Marie's parents to their home for the holiday.

"Merry Christmas!" Scott shouted as he opened the door. His voice boomed through the house.

Abigail vacated her spot beside Dorothy, where they were rolling out cookie dough together, and ran to the front hall. "Grandpa!"

Scott swept her up in his arms, showering her with kisses and tears he could not hold back. No sooner had she been smothered by him than she squirmed away to embrace her grandma's waist.

"I've missed you," Abigail said.

"Oh my, child," Clara responded, wiping the tears from her own eyes. "Step back, and let me see how grown up you've become."

Abigail stood straight and stepped back, holding her head high.

"Wow, it has been a long time indeed," Clara stated.

David had stopped at the top of the stairs and watched the moment unfold before him. Tears stung his eyes too, but he ignored them and walked down to join the group.

"David." Scott shot out his hand, which David also ignored.

He stepped forward and embraced his father-in-law and friend, after which he turned to Clara and hugged her tightly, not letting go until he was sure she knew how much he cared.

David's heart had changed over these past few months. He was ready, willing, and excited to work with God for his purposes. He constantly remembered the words God impressed on him throughout his life—compassion and unconditional love. He realized that God, the creator of all and the one that knows all, spoke those words to him, created those traits in him, and planned David's use of them long before their use was necessary. Regardless of what was to become of him or his family, good or bad, God had a plan. David trusted him.

David, Clara, and Scott had spent many nights talking over the phone since this revelation sank in. David openly shared all he had withheld, all that had transpired with Marie. He also shared his concerns of Abigail's mental health, and sure enough, her behavior seemed very similar to that of Marie's when she was little. Again, this was something David was leaving in the Lord's hands. Regardless of her future, he was called to love her unconditionally.

Cameron became very involved in their lives. His visit in mid-August enlightened David. It also humbled him since the negativity and judgment he was expecting had never existed. Cam, through the legislature, had supported the many hours of work invested by a group of people devoted to better mental health care in their state. The State Hospital at Raleigh was a direct result of this work.

David led his in-laws to the kitchen. "Dorothy," he called, "I'd like to introduce you to Abigail's grandparents, Mr. and Mrs. Tudor."

Dorothy turned from the counter and wiped her hands on her apron. She reached out to shake the hands of those that were outstretched to her. "Nice to meet you," she repeated too many times.

"Abigail, could you help Dorothy finish the cookies?"

A smile spread across her face, and she got back up on the stool she had been on prior to company arriving. "Of course, Daddy. I'd love to."

"Thank you," David said.

Clara and Scott joined David in the living room where the Christmas tree stood bare, waiting for their time to decorate it together.

"Thank you so much, David, for having us here," Clara said.

"I couldn't have imagined a better way to spend our holiday. You're the best gift."

"How's Marie?"

"I visited her last week," David said. "I've not seen her really awake yet. They keep her sedated to keep her safe. It's a new treatment they're trying."

"Oh my goodness, David, that seems so wrong," Clara said.

"I felt the same way. Now, with Cam's support and those he's been working with, the doctors at the State Hospital are open to allow Marie and I to be part of an experiment I've suggested."

"That sounds terrible, an experiment. What does that mean?" Scott asked. "I can't even understand what she's going through. How can you seem so accepting? What if they're holding her there and sedating her without need? We took care of Clara's mother at home."

David looked at the couple and recognized their point of view. He had it himself, but they were so angry that they couldn't listen to what he was trying to tell them. They were in denial and highly judgmental of the care their child was receiving.

"We'd like to see her," Scott said. "Before we return home."

David knew that seeing her was going to make them even more distraught, but there was nothing he could do to change that. He decided to stop sharing his plans for Marie, because he knew doing so would be fruitless.

"You can follow me there on your way back home after Christmas. I'll take you in to see her."

After the cookies were taken from the oven, David drove Dorothy home so she could share the Christmas holiday with her family. Clara and Scott stayed with Abigail, spending time reconnecting before the four of them decorated the Christmas tree. The night was magical even though David felt disconnected. Through countless phone conversations he'd failed to anticipate this reaction.

Christmas day was simple. The few presents under the tree were enough for Abigail who was more excited to spend time with her grandparents. The day after Christmas, Dorothy returned to be with Abigail, and David drove to Raleigh with his in-laws following.

After passing through the State Hospital's gate, David parked, and they walked up the stairs and through the grand front doors together. He watched them in interest as he approached the check-in desk. He could sense their hope but knew disappointment would soon be experienced.

"Hi, Mrs. Stevens. I have Clara and Scott Tudor with me to see my wife."

"Thank you, Mr. Towell. A nurse will be right with you. You can have a seat in the waiting area."

David went in to the waiting area, a space to the left of the main doors that held a half-dozen comfortable seats and some outdated magazines for the rare few who bothered to visit.

He had little to say. The quiet between them felt strange.

After twenty awkward minutes, a nurse arrived to lead them to Marie's dorm. David walked ahead of them. She was his wife, and he felt responsible for any exposure of her and her situation. After entering the large familiar room, he walked to his wife's bed and kissed her gently on her cheek. He whispered of his love close to her ear. She was sound asleep and unaware of the special Christmas visitors she had.

The couple stood in front of Marie's bed, shocked. They looked at their daughter, who was a shadow of who she'd been, and then at the many patients assigned to the beds in the room around her. The sounds of moaning, the distant stares, and the lack of normalcy, under the guise of a hospital, overwhelmed their parental expectations.

No amount of discussion could have prepared them for this. David knew that. He had expected this reaction. It had been his initially as well. The image appeared frightening to outsiders, but this facility offered humanity and a home to those suffering with mental illness. It was a far cry from the previous thousand or so years during which the afflicted were persecuted, killed, and maimed.

David realized the blessing he and Marie were receiving, merely by the period of time in history in which they lived, and he was thankful. He gazed down upon her and, with these thoughts in mind, loved her all the more. God was good, they were blessed, and David was looking forward to their future.

CHAPTER

37

Earlier, in November, Cameron Morrison had introduced David to Fredrick Allen and Martha Hobbs, representatives of the State Hospital of Raleigh. They had spent many years in the field of mental health, and their research was considered groundbreaking. Cam was hoping David would feel better about the care of his wife and the facility she was now in if he heard some of the amazing information Cam had been privy to as a state dignitary. The work being done at the state hospital was widely supported by North Carolina's government since its inception in the late 1800s. The treatment of those who struggled with mental illness was being transformed in the country; the State Hospital of Raleigh was one of the best.

Fear of the mentally ill, who acted or appeared different, was being replaced with compassion. Aggression toward those once considered demon possessed was subsiding, and newer, humane treatments were being explored and offered.

David had met them when his heart was heavy. It was important, he agreed, to listen to the information and research they had spent years working on. They were passionate about their beliefs and discoveries, but in their excitement of the large picture, he felt they were missing the smaller, more intimate one, the person afflicted.

Marie was a woman, a wife, and a mother. She was loved and had given love. Now, as far as he was being told, she was no longer going to be the woman he fell in love with and was fortunate to marry. She was no longer going to sit on the couch late into the night beside him, laughing at his jokes. She was never again going to make dinner while sharing conversation with him. She was no longer going to go horseback riding and have picnics. She was no longer going to participate in raising their little girl, the little girl they had been teaching their morals, values, and life lessons to. She was sedated for being different, deep sleep therapy, they called it, a method being used by a Swiss psychiatrist and one they were excited to try out here in America.

She was not their experiment; she was his wife. He was absorbing the great advances in treatment of the mentally ill, but they were sorely missing the mark in his life. He wanted his wife.

It was after these discussions that he began hearing God's direction. He recognized his attempts at being in control were fruitless. He was also able to see that God's plan was bigger than the traditional family life of humanity. The passion of those David had met with ignited a need in him to become involved, and he suggested an experiment, one of simpler living.

After sharing his ideas with Mr. Allen and Mrs. Hobbs, Cam encouraged David to present them at the state house and seek funding. It took months of presentations to ignite the same excitement in a larger population of influence.

While David was running with God's plan in the legislature, he was also working with the state hospital staff preparing to reconnect with Marie. Though she was expected to be different than the woman he'd married, he was excited to get to know her.

Their relationship would now be unequal. For him to care for Marie with the unconditional love of a husband, David needed to keep Christ, first and foremost, at his center. He did not want to risk becoming intolerant. He wanted to be confident that frustration and irritation would not be able to take root because that could lead to condescending behavior toward her.

Lord, please help me to be compassionate and love Marie unconditionally. As soon as that prayer left his heart, David was overcome with emotion.

David, I raised you and planned for your compassionate heart. I allowed the lessons you've endured and gave you the tools to embrace the ability to love unconditionally. You're never alone on this journey. These are my traits, which I'm living through you. Marie's my child, who I gave to be your wife. If you remain close to me, you will not falter. Don't fear. The words were audible and powerful.

David had direction and, with that direction, did not fear the outcome. He wanted his wife home, and believed God was going to make that happen.

All the skills David used in creating and growing businesses in his lifetime came to play during this effort. He met with politicians. He endured the attacks of those opposed to humane treatment of the mentally ill. He saw how powerful fear was.

For more than a thousand years, fear fueled the desire to eradicate people with these disabilities, yet now, during such a period of change as new as this, Marie lived. God had to have allowed that, David thought. Clara had chosen to care for her mentally ill mother in the privacy of her home. That choice avoided the focus of society, which, during those years, would have brought strife upon their family.

If Marie's grandmother's illness had been public knowledge, if Clara and Scott had not left the life they loved to care for her, society might have dictated a different outcome. It hadn't been many years earlier that the offspring of schizophrenic people were made sterile, whether they showed signs of the illness or not; it was hereditary, after all. Abigail would not have been conceived. Would he even have considered Marie a prospective partner had he understood the family history?

Due to David's great efforts, approval was granted, in the spring of 1932, for the state to purchase a dilapidated building in Raleigh and have it refurbished and used as a transitional home for some who were mentally ill. This approval put some people back to work during the depression and gave hope to families willing to become caretakers and support loved ones suffering with mental illness in their own homes. Moving them out of state funded facilities would save tax dollars. It was a win-win situation.

David spearheaded the idea and was declaring he was ready and willing to care for his wife at home. This was a route to achieve some sort of normalcy for both the family and the patient.

There would be requirements; patients and families would be screened, and only those determined to be low risk would transfer to the transition house. Mental health classes would be required for all involved while there. These classes would teach the long, sordid history of mental illness and all the latest medications and therapies available. After the patient is able to transition home, they and their caretakers would be required to attend regular meetings, to stay connected with the ever-changing world of mental health care and to ensure a doctor has regular contact.

David visited Marie daily in preparation for their future. Not only was he husband and best friend but would hopefully be her caretaker, if all went well. Their experiences during this process were going to be the blueprint for the hospital to follow with other families.

During this time, he witnessed the behaviors of patients at the hospital experiencing vast levels of psychosis. Being in their midst helped David understand them better. In time, he stopped seeing them as mentally ill patients and began to see them as people.

Though the State Hospital at Raleigh was at capacity, they provided David a bed beside Marie's to use while the doctors slowly brought her out of the sleep coma they had induced. It had been half a year since she had been taken from their home in an ambulance. It had been that long since he had seen her awake enough to be verbal. David felt excited, yet prayed for strength to accept her, however different she might be when she woke up.

Initially, as the drugs were being reduced, Marie moaned a lot and rolled around as if she were uncomfortable. David fought the sometimes-overwhelming feeling of being alarmed. After a day or so, she began to talk to herself, seemingly unaware that he was present. Nothing she said made sense; much of it was mumbled without any semblance of words. He moved his bed as close to hers as he could and held her hand whenever she moved. He wanted to be sure she knew she was not alone.

On the third morning, while the nurses were getting some of their wards ready to go to the dining room for breakfast, David felt Marie tense up beside him. He sat up on his elbow and looked at her. She was lying down and rigid; her eyes were open, and they were looking around in alarm as if searching for something, anything familiar. David leaned in to her view, but though there was some flicker of recognition, she did not relax.

"Marie," David whispered close to her face. "Marie, honey, I'm here."

She turned her head very slowly toward him but kept looking around, as if fearful. "David, they got us," she whispered. "I tried to stop them. I'm sorry."

Many scenarios had passed through his head during this long ordeal. Thankfully, this had been one of them. "I know, honey, but it turned out they had some good intentions."

"No, they don't." She struggled to sit up as she looked around. Her body was frail and weak, not used to moving quickly. A nurse stepped forward ready to help, causing Marie to turn back toward David and whisper, "Where's Abigail? What did they do with her?"

"Oh no, they didn't get her. She's at home waiting to see you."

"Home. Where'd they take us?" She was leaning in and speaking low as if she was afraid the nurse would hear their conversation.

David felt sadness kick in because of her odd behavior and her gaunt appearance. *My God, please help me stay out of that place of sadness. I can't be of any help there. Please give me strength. Help me live for today and not look backward.*

He didn't want to give in to missing his wife, who she used to be. His calling was to love her for who she was and would be. He felt peace within and smiled, reaching up to caress his wife's face as he attempted to soothe her fear.

"Honey, its fine. Everything'll be all right. I'm here with you, and we're going to be fine."

She lay back down, curled up on her side facing her husband, and accepted his affections as the commotion of hospital life went on around them.

CHAPTER

38

The transition house had generated a lot of controversy, due largely to public perception. The other issue was its location. David fought for this project to be located in an upscale business neighborhood. He wanted it clearly understood that mental illness did not discriminate, and a family choosing to support their own loved one, choosing to take on the burden themselves rather than relying on the tax payers, should not be made to feel like they were low class or undesirable.

A project such as this should not take place, he argued, in a place where poverty and crime rates were high. He wanted families to be able to go for walks in safe neighborhoods while they were in the city training. He insisted their visits to the city should be visually pleasing and uplifting, not disparaging.

David had been traveling back and forth between home, the state hospital, and the capitol building for eight months now, and with the transition housing renovation nearly complete, he had a lot of work ahead of him in the city. It only made sense to rent an apartment there. The time in transition for each family would be different, based on a case-by-case basis. David had no idea how long his family's transition might take, and he had been away from Abigail too much as it was.

Dorothy was watching her during the day, and Pastor Steve's wife was staying at the house the nights David wasn't able to get home. He rented the top apartment in a secured building next door to the transition house. After meeting with Dorothy's mother, it was agreed that Dorothy could live in the city to take care of Abigail until Marie moved into the transition house, where childcare would be provided.

"Wow, Daddy, that was scary," Abigail said about the elevator ride up, but as soon as she entered the apartment, her face brightened. "This is really neat!" She walked around, looking into each room.

"Dorothy, I hope you don't mind, I set you up in Abigail's room with her."

Dorothy entered the bedroom she would share and walked around in a big circle. "Mr. Towell, I don't mind at all. It's bigger than both the girls' room and boys' room put together in my house." She watched as Abigail ran past her and jumped up onto a bed. "I guess this one's mine, then," Dorothy said, walking up to the other bed and fingering the coverlet. "I don't have my own bed at home neither. We share," she said quietly. She turned back toward David. "Thank you, Mr. Towell."

David smiled. "You're welcome, Dorothy. Now listen, girls. I'm heading out to check on the transition house next door, and I've got a meeting scheduled with someone in a couple hours. Do you think you're all set? I'll be back for dinner."

"Okay, Daddy," Abigail said before continuing her exploration.

"Dorothy, do you think you'll be okay here? I know the city's different than what you're used to."

"Yes, Mr. Towell. I'm good."

"Okay then." He headed to the elevator. "I'll be back later, girls!"

Over the following month, David spent many hours walking the streets, introducing himself to people, and visiting the businesses around the transition house as it was being renovated. His name was well known, and he was respected in Raleigh. He used his status to educate those around him. He wanted people to step away from fear, and if connecting mental illness to the life of a person they felt they knew, liked, and trusted made any difference, then David was happy to share.

The state hospital had met with a number of patients and families they thought might be good candidates for transition, and in early May, ten patients moved, including Marie.

Marie acted different. She was childlike now. While at the state hospital, David had spent hours every day with her but chose to not have Abigail become involved until Marie moved to the transition house. He was concerned she would be overwhelmed by the magnitude of so many ill people in one place, as her grandparents had. He got to know many of them and had become close to a few. He was generally accepted in their hospital community, which is what he wanted to achieve to really gain a deep understanding for what they were going through.

During the first week Marie was living next door, David didn't say anything to the girls. It wasn't time yet for Dorothy to go home, but it would be soon. He helped Marie get settled in and continued getting to know her and regaining her trust. The love she had for him was evident, and it hadn't seemed clear that she realized life had permanently changed for them. David supposed he had to really pray about that for himself. How much of it had to change?

"David, when can we go home? I miss living with you and Abigail. I couldn't wait to get away from there. It was creepy, but now, you let them put me somewhere else. Why do I have to live somewhere else? Let's just go home," she said.

"I know, Marie. I understand your impatience, but you've gone through a rough time. We've been meeting with the psychologists. You understand the diagnosis, don't you?"

"I do. It's not as bad as they're telling you. Don't believe them, David. I'm not a freak like my grandmother was."

"Marie, that's not fair. You know what schizophrenia is. It is likely that this is what your grandmother suffered with. I know you understand, and I hope I've shown you this is something we're working on together. I want to be sure we live a happy and safe life together. That'll only happen if we can learn and openly share all we can."

He turned Marie's face toward him again since she had looked away as a defiant child would. "I love you and am just as anxious as you to have us all home again, but I want to be sure we do it right so we don't end up with anyone hurt again."

"You understand, don't you?" she said. "I thought they were using Pastor Steve to get to us. I'm really sorry I screwed it up."

It was discussions like this that made Marie appear meek, not defensive or embarrassed, but timid and shy. He wasn't sure she was going to trust him fully. He wanted them to just live their life, simple and unashamed.

"Honey, its fine. There's no need to be sorry. We're learning a lot because of what happened, and that's good. Now"—David chose to change the subject, a tactic he was realizing was going to be important in their lives—"Abigail's going to be five soon, you know."

It worked. She was excited and thinking of their daughter. "Can I see Abigail soon?"

David smiled. "Yes, we've been waiting until we have the right amount of nurses before offering child care. The last nurse joined us yesterday."

"Child care. What do you mean?"

"There'll be a number of families visiting regularly, and that would certainly mean children are going to need to be watched, so we decided to hire staff for that."

Marie listened, seeming suspicious. After a few minutes, she spoke up accusingly, "You're talking like you planned to do this, to have me live here, to have other people bring their children here."

In an instant, a conversation meant to bring excitement, excitement that she was going to be reunited with her daughter, turned into Marie trying to figure out a deeper, sinister plan.

David shook his head. "Honey, I did plan all this. I planned it for people like us, families that want to be together. They can come to this place, and learn how to be a family again. I know you may not understand, but it was all for good reasons. Nothing bad is happening here. I'm sorry if I've confused you. Now, about Abigail."

Marie's face brightened once more as David continued.

"I'm planning to bring you to her."

"Home? I'm going home?" Marie became excited, and David suddenly felt weary of the conversation. "Marie. I'm not bringing you home." He realized he had to speak in the present and decided to wait and let her know of the meeting with Abigail as it was happening, instead. "Tomorrow morning, I'll come and see you. Right now, I've got to go." He leaned in to kiss her. "I love you."

David returned to the apartment and spent the rest of the afternoon with Abigail and Dorothy. He explained to his soon-to-be five-year-old daughter that she would see her mother in the morning. He was bringing Marie up to the apartment to have lunch with them. He wanted to be sure Abigail understood her mommy was very different now.

"I know, Daddy. You've said that before. It's okay. I can't wait to hug her."

David couldn't wait either. He was excited when he went to bed.

CHAPTER

39

"How are you feeling today?" David asked Marie.

"I'm good. Why?" she asked suspiciously.

David thought her paranoia was understandable after all she'd been through. Like the Bible suggested, what she feared the most came upon her. She was afraid someone was coming to get Abigail, and in that fear, she made it all happen, except she was the one who ended up waking up in a different place.

"I want to be sure you're feeling good is all." He reached for her hand, and Marie stood up. He bowed. "May I have this dance, my dear?"

Marie looked around and giggled shyly, much like the girl she had been long ago. He stepped up to her and took her hand in his and wrapped his other arm around the small of her back and started dancing. She followed along without hesitation but questioned him just the same.

"David, there's no music."

"But I'm sure I hear it softly." He started to hum close to her ear.

She smiled. Miss Sidney walked by them with a tight smile on her lips. In the time the transition house had been open, David could count on one hand the smiles he saw that woman show. He was feeling like today was magic, though, and nothing could bring him down. He was bringing Marie home, not the home she was looking for, but it was his space, just the same. Abigail was waiting excitedly.

"David, you don't like to dance," Marie said slowly, as if she was trying to pull a memory out of the recesses of her mind.

"Oh, but you do, my dear."

"Yes, I do," she responded. "I do."

David danced her out of the large room and into the front lobby, where he nodded to the male nurse they had hired. There was a short supply of male nurses, the pay was not terribly good, so Derek was a find. David felt it was important to have a man tending the lobby. He was dressed like a doorman.

At first blush, the atmosphere remained consistent with the surrounding buildings that employed doormen. Derek's job, however, was much more critical to the success of the transition house. He was trained to look for any sign of potential trouble in the patients as they were preparing to go out for walks with family or returning from the community. All of the research indicated that psychotic outbreaks were handled best if caught early. Visual signs of distress might be missed by family members not yet in tune.

David had already arranged to take Marie out of the building. Derek nodded in response, then held the door for the couple.

"Where are we going?" Marie asked as they went down the marble steps.

"You'll be seeing Abigail today. We've been staying here," David explained as he pointed up at the neighboring building.

The pair walked through a parking lot and crossed the lawn. When they reached the front of the building, a doorman nodded to David and held the door open.

"Marty, this is my wife, Marie." David turned toward his wife. "Marie, this is my doorman, Marty."

"Nice to meet you, ma'am," Marty said as he bowed low.

Marie smiled. "Thank you, nice to meet you too."

David was worried how she would handle the social world, but she seemed to be doing fine. He led her to the elevator, where they rode together alone. She looked nervous. David hugged her tightly, and she relaxed.

"I love you, Marie. Don't be nervous. Abigail's excited to see you."

"What must she be thinking of me? Her mother's crazy."

David held her back from him briefly so he could look in her eyes. "You're not crazy. She misses you and loves you." He held her close again as they continued up to the apartment.

When the elevator door opened, Marie's eyes brightened at the sight of her daughter, and she stepped out quickly with arms opened wide. "Oh, Abigail!" she exclaimed.

David watched as Abigail ran into her mother's embrace. They held each other a long time, both crying.

———⁓⁓⁕⁜⁓⁜⁓⁜⁓⁕⁓⁓———

As the month wore on, the family worked together through some intense mental health teaching. Scott and Clara joined them for some of the classes. The months since they'd last seen Marie were tough. They were horrified at her condition and very angry at David. He allowed them their space but had Abigail call them regularly, knowing their differences should not affect her relationship with them. In late spring, they became aware of what David was doing and called him one night, asking for his forgiveness. They had heard of the transition house and his call for support through their local newspaper.

He assured them he had no hard feelings, he was just glad they were becoming part of their lives again. He understood their concerns and appreciated their love for their daughter.

Marie's behavior remained stable, outside of a few times she became unrealistically concerned about "them" and what "they" were going to do, which caused the nurses and David to be a little more alert. The art of redirection became much more fine-tuned.

With Abigail taken care of at the transition house and Marie doing well, David resumed his meetings with Cam in search of ways to reinvigorate the economy. He became a spokesman for financial balance. At least that was his goal. He spoke at churches throughout Raleigh, encouraging others to follow more closely the concept of financial balance and freedom from debt, which had kept him afloat during the difficult days after the stock market crash and the present bank closures.

He encouraged others to find a trust and faith in God on a personal, intimate level, regardless of situation. The speaking engagements led to discussions with individuals who wanted to understand his trust in and devotion to God in the face of the mental health difficulties his family was so publicly facing.

David kept close to God, constantly seeking his guidance and wisdom during these discussions. He was an example to others of the peace that could be experienced with trust and obedience.

As part of their transition work, David was able to bring Marie to the apartment for dinner dates while Abigail remained at the transition house. He did the cooking in the beginning, but soon, they were cooking together, adding to their closeness. The comfortable intimacy of their relationship was returning. In some ways it was deeper than before, yet it was different; they were different people now. Romance seemed to linger in the air at times, which David felt unsure of.

He lay in bed one night, praying about their relationship and where the line should be between his original role of husband and lover and his present role as caretaker.

The changes in David and Marie's relationship were mostly felt in the area of communication. The amount of general conversation became less, words that David said needed to hold absolute meaning. Marie's confusion was kept more to a minimum when less abstract discussion was introduced.

When she became involved in chatting or mumbling for no obvious reason, which happened often, David chose to allow it and only redirected if she became agitated. After all, he wondered, was it something he should become upset about? If there were battles to choose, trying to make her normal appearing or sounding wasn't one of them. He loved her for who she was.

In the process of realizing this and living it, David recognized also that she should not feel shunned as his wife. The revelation of this, as it sank in, was deep. He imagined the confusion and insecurity he would cause her if he turned her away romantically.

When God brings people together to love and unite, that is the most vulnerable time of giving; it is the ultimate moment of trust. To turn her away when faced with that moment would destroy any confidence she may have gained. She was trying to resume her place in the home. She was working toward being a mother again. She was trying to be a wife, and though there were many times of disconnect, those times of clarity needed to be honored.

June was upon them. It was warm out, and the weather was enjoyable. David invited Marie on a date. They went for a walk around the city and stopped at a couple of shops to pick up items to make dinner at the apartment. David held her hand as they walked and watched her whenever they talked. She was clear in her thinking for the most part, and he was glad for the times she was. When they reached the apartment, they worked together, making dinner and laughing over funny memories from the past.

When dinner was done being cooked, they sat across from each other at the table and enjoyed the comfortable silence as they ate. After dinner, Marie stood at the sink doing the dishes like it was natural.

David watched her as he thought about their lives together. He went to her and snaked his arms around her waist from behind. "I love you, Marie," he whispered in her ear.

She chuckled and spun around to face him, placing her dripping hands on his shoulders, getting him intentionally wet.

"Hey," he said as he pulled away, looking at his wet shirt. "What was that for?"

She laughed, and in that moment, David was happy God had kept them together and showed them how to be a family still. Marie began pulling his shirt up.

"What are you doing?" he asked in surprise.

"I think you're wet," she said teasingly. "And you should get undressed."

David felt butterflies fill his stomach. His look turned solemn, and briefly, he felt unsure. She stepped forward and kissed him intimately. After some second thoughts about the decision to trust what he had felt God telling him, he led her to the bedroom.

CHAPTER

40

David had stayed late working with Cam. He felt guilty leaving Abigail for so long, but they were making progress. They had been meeting with owners of businesses that were on the threshold of closing their doors and helped them to reconstruct their financial outlook. They taught them how to consolidate debt and reviewed their assets and liabilities to see where wiser choices could be made. Each business they helped to remain open, through reorganization of what they already had, saved the jobs of many employees, which translated into less stress and more security for that many more families.

It was getting late, though, and David packed up to head back to the transition house. Abigail's fifth birthday was tomorrow, and she was excited. Her birthday wish was to go back to the house at Minnesott Beach, but the doctors felt Marie was not ready to return to the old life yet. The two of them made an agreement that they would spend the morning with Marie and head to the ocean just after lunch.

Abigail was excited that she was going to sleep in her old bed again, and she was going to see Charlie. They could ride on the beach and make sand sculptures again. It was going to be difficult leaving Marie for a couple of days, but it would make a great gift for Abigail.

David arrived at the transition house at quarter to seven. As Derek held the door open for him, he saw his wife hurrying to meet him. She was dressed up in a beautiful pale yellow gown. With her hair up and the soft wisps touching her beaming face, he could not help but smile. She was beautiful.

"Where've you been?" she asked. "The reunion's been well under way, and our friends have been wondering if you're really coming, though I keep telling them what a busy man you are." Marie reached up to embrace him.

As the faint smell of her perfume reached his nose, he looked at Derek. They both saw it clearly. He loved this woman, even when she was in the midst of her own psychosis.

He kissed her. "I was just now able to get away from the office. I'm sorry if I've kept you waiting. I didn't know there was a reunion taking place tonight. Please forgive me." He smiled down at Marie and felt a tug of sadness overwhelm him. She had been doing so well, but rather than call attention to her state of mind, David played along with the behavior. He felt it may help her move out of it.

"How's Abigail? Is she enjoying the festivities?"

"Oh yes. I think so anyway. Miss Sidney is with her." Marie leaned in closer to her husband and whispered, "You know, I don't much like her. I think she's putting bad ideas into our daughter's head. Perhaps I should have her replaced." Marie became quiet then and appeared lost in thought.

Watching Marie in quiet moments such as this made David wish he could understand what she was thinking. What was really going on inside her busy mind?

Marie suddenly snapped her head up to look at David. "What time is it?"

Pulling his coat sleeve back to see the face of his watch, he answered his wife's hurried question with a calculatedly calm response. "Mmm, it's nearly seven." And raising his eyes to meet hers, he inquired, "Why? What is it?"

Marie turned to Derek, who was standing in the entryway, and smiled at him before grasping David's hand. She looked up at him with a crafty look in her eyes. "Come, let's be quick."

Derek, who was ready to intervene, looked to David for direction, but when David nodded at him and winked, he stepped back from the doorway. Marie opened the door, pulled her ball gown up within her free hand, and tugged David into a trot as they raced down the marble stairs and across the parking lot. Reaching the grass, she continued her explanation but did not slow her pace at all.

"Miss Sidney, she has to leave by eight. There's not much time left."

David caught her flirting glance and couldn't help but allow it to have the intended effect.

They arrived at his apartment building in minutes, where the doorman smiled, tipped his hat, and held the door open wide for the familiar couple. David and Marie entered the elevator. Marie giggled as she pushed the button that would lead them to his apartment. David watched her face and smiled when she looked back at him.

"I love you, Marie," David said, feeling emotional and unsure of what he should do.

Marie smiled in response. Her beauty radiated, and it brought a quickening to his heart. He offered the struggle he was feeling up to the heavens. *Lord, this is my wife, whom I love unconditionally. I am going to love her even now.*

"Thanks. I love you too." David heard her words and felt that it was God's confirmation to not worry. He watched a blush rise to Marie's cheeks as she quickly glanced up at the numbers, which were ascending.

"Here we are." She always announced that right before the bell rang; it was like a game to her. It seemed to take all of her attention as she would stare at the changing numbers, but she very rarely missed her cue. The elevator door opened.

"What time is it, David?" Marie's voice was rushed, and though she was smiling, he could sense the concern.

After a glance at his watch, he responded, "It's just after seven."

"Oh no, come. We must hurry." Marie pulled him to the doorway of his bedroom. "There's not much time. Here, help me with this, please." She turned her back to him and held her head to the side as David unzipped the back of her gown.

Shrugging out of the sleeves, she dropped the gown to the floor and climbed onto the four-poster bed.

"Come, honey." She smiled and patted the space beside her.

The couple returned to the transition house just in time to face a very irritated Miss Sidney. David helped their little girl put the puzzle away she had been working on then spent the rest of their time relaxing together in the great room before it was time for David to bring Abigail home.

"Honey, I'm sorry, but we have to leave now. It's getting late for Abigail. We'll see you in the morning," David said to Marie.

"Mommy, it's my birthday tomorrow," Abigail excitedly said.

David expected that she had repeated those words a million times.

"Really, Abigail, that's very exciting," Marie responded, sounding like she cared but didn't really understand.

David kissed his wife goodnight as the nurse came to bring her nighttime medicine.

Abigail's birthday was upon them, and she was as excited as any brand-new five-year-old girl could be. She skipped around the apartment as David made pancakes, which was a treat she had requested. After all, this was going to be a day directed by the fair lady herself. She settled at the table and started coloring with her new crayons.

"What are you working on, princess?"

Abigail smiled at the name. "I'm making Mommy a birthday card."

David wandered over to the table and looked over Abigail's shoulder at the picture she was making of Marie's horse. "It's your birthday, silly. Why are you making a card for Mommy?"

"Because she doesn't always know what things mean, and I want her to feel like this day is special for her."

David smiled. "Well, that's very kind of you, and you know, I think that actually makes sense." David was impressed.

"See, I'm drawing Duplin because I want her to remember him and be excited that she'll see him again soon."

David was caught by her words. He was unsure about the next move in their lives. He was able to work now, because both of his ladies were cared for all day. The psychologist said Marie was doing well, and he liked how David responded to her when she wandered in and out of the odd traits of schizophrenia. He felt David's reactions actually kept her in check. Their observations of him helped them guide other families which were achieving similar results. The medications she was on were minimal, but it was imperative to continue them.

David agreed with that and was glad she was progressing, but he didn't know how he could give up the work he was involved with now for the state. He was scheduled to speak at least once weekly, and the effects of the work he and Cam had been doing were starting to make a difference in a lot of people's lives.

It would be difficult for him to scale back his activities at this point to stay home and take care of his family. He was helping so many people, and the care at the transition house was convenient to him. In his heart he knew this was wrong. There was a purpose for the transition house. How could he, of all people, take advantage of it? His internal struggle was difficult.

CHAPTER

41

It felt good to be home, David realized. They did all they had set out to do on this busy birthday. They visited with Marie for lunch, rode the horse and pony down the beach and back, made a huge birthday cake sand sculpture, and now they were relaxing.

David was struggling, though. Balance was not there for him. He lounged in a beach chair facing the water, taking in the warm ocean breeze. He absentmindedly watched Abigail as she played but was thinking of the next struggling business he was scheduled to work with in Raleigh. After some time, Abigail's chattering penetrated his thoughts. He realized it sounded familiar, oddly familiar.

He focused on his daughter now and watched her as she played. His heart dropped when he heard her simple chatter change, she was now answering questions that nobody was asking, something he'd heard Marie do a lot before her breakdown.

David returned his attention to the vastness of the ocean, soul searching as Abigail played about the beach. He ignored her imaginary discussions and felt detached. He thought about his wife struggling with her own illness. David was feeling convicted. He knew his role was to care for his family. At what point had he turned the focus to himself and the good he was doing again for others? Where was the compassion he had for his own loved ones? As he sat in a state of deep self-reflection, Abigail climbed over the sand dunes.

Abigail felt like she was having an amazing day. This was the best birthday ever! She was able to spend time with Mommy and ride Charlie again. He seemed excited to see her. She got to build in the sand with her daddy again as they made a great birthday cake with five candles. It felt like forever since they had done something like that, and to top off this great day, she was going to sleep in her old bed, in her own room again. She missed being home.

"Abigail."

She looked up from her sand tools but couldn't find the woman who called her name. She looked at her dad to see if he noticed, but he was just looking out at the ocean.

"Abigail."

She heard it again. "Did you hear that?" she asked in a whispered voice in case anyone else could help her.

"It came from over there," was the response from a boy who'd just climbed over the dune.

Abigail looked around. "But I don't know where you mean."

"Abigail."

She heard it again.

Another voice chimed in, "We're over here. Can you help us?"

Abigail continued the conversation with the boy in a quiet voice. "My dad's been awful busy," she explained. "Let's be quiet. I don't want to bother him. What kind of help do they need? Did you see what they want?"

After a bit of discussion, she decided to climb over the sand dune and down to the rocky shore to see what was going on for herself.

"Abigail. Come help us."

"There you are," she responded to a group of people standing by a rowboat that was lying on the rocks.

"Honey, we need your help. Can you get us out onto the water?"

Abigail instantly liked them. They were old, and of course, old people really liked little girls. They commented on what she was wearing and how sweet she was. Abigail smiled and was glad to help.

"Just get the boat in the water so we can get in," the lady in the polka-dot dress said.

"She's too little to do that," a tiny old man with a pouty face said.

Abigail stood tall and proud. "I'm five, just today. It's my birthday."

"Happy birthday," the group said in unison.

"Well then, that probably does mean she's strong enough to help," the man answered with a toothless smile.

Abigail pushed and pulled and worked until the boat made its way to the water's edge.

"Oh, okay, everyone. Let's get in," the lady said.

The group of five old and frail men and women helped each other climb into the boat. Their feet were getting wet, and the tiny man took his shoes off after sitting in the boat to shake the water out. Abigail laughed.

"Okay, Abigail, push us out into deeper water. I think we're stuck on the rocks."

"Push you?" Abigail asked. "You might be too heavy for me to push."

"Well now, girl, you must try. We're too old to be getting in and out and in again."

"Okay." She took a deep breath and pushed on the back of the boat until it budged a little. She went up to the front and pulled on the bow a bit and lost her footing as it moved.

"That's it. Keep it up."

She smiled with pride. She really was bigger now that she was five. She returned to the back and pushed until it finally was fully afloat.

"Come on now," the woman in the front seat said. "Come along with us."

"What do you mean?" Abigail asked. "There's no more room."

"Well then, just hold on to the side and swim. That'll get us where we're going," a woman in the third row suggested.

As the boat started floating away, Abigail had to make up her mind.

"Come on. We'll be gettin' too far for you soon, sweetie. Come take hold."

Abigail wandered into the ocean up to her middle and then lunged out to grab hold of the boat.

"There you go, dearie. You made it," said a woman in the front seat with a big floppy hat on.

Abigail smiled and used her free arm to compel them forward. "Where should we be going?" she asked, feeling a little out of breath.

"Oh, just over there."

She looked to see where the gentleman was pointing but missed seeing the direction.

"Dearie, come here. I need to tell you something," the floppy-hatted woman called.

Abigail was feeling tired and looked at the woman in the front seat. "I can't. I have to hold on."

"Sure you can, dearie. It's a secret I've got to tell you. Come on up here. Swim. I have to whisper it to you," she coaxed.

Abigail didn't want to hurt her feelings, so she let go of the boat and tried to swim to her but suddenly realized she couldn't. She reached up to hold the side of the boat again, but nothing was there to hold. Panic hit her. Her heart was pounding, and she pulled her head up from the water in a desperate search for something to hold on to. The empty boat was floating off out of reach. Abigail floundered, but only briefly.

David went into the house, realizing he had become absorbed in his own struggles. Today wasn't about him or the struggles mental illness was putting him through. It was a special day for his beautiful daughter. He pulled the cake out from its hiding place on top of the refrigerator and set it on the counter. He placed five pink candles in it and had the matches ready to do their magic.

"Abigail!"

He listened for her footsteps from upstairs but didn't hear them. He went to the bottom of the staircase and hollered again but heard nothing. He went back to the door through which he had just come and looked about.

"Abigail!" he shouted, but there was no response.

He went to the main door, wondering if she had gone to the paddock. He could see Charlie out in the field but did not see her. Where had she gone? He wandered the house, not feeling any sense of urgency, and ultimately settled in the window of his own bedroom to look outside.

Lord, where can she be?

Her new pink outfit caught his eye. "No! No, no, Abigail."

David turned and ran down the stairs, slipping down the last third of them and regaining his footing at the bottom as he ran screaming back out the door he had come in earlier. He scrambled over the dunes, his heart pounding in his chest. He fell repeatedly on the uneven boulders that rose up between him and the ocean. He did not feel the scratches he received as he flailed his way into the water.

"Abigail!" he screamed as he clawed at the water to reach her. When his hand caught on the fabric of her dress, he pulled her to him and fought the current back to the shore where he curled her up into his lap and sought for life.

"No!" he cried out in anguish, yelling to the heavens above. "No!"

CHAPTER

42

The funeral was difficult. The small casket, the flowers draping it, the emptiness of standing alone before it, it was the worst thing David could have ever imagined living through. His heart was broken, and his spirit was empty. He didn't want to live through this.

Haven't I endured enough, Lord? Believe me when I say I have! Why, why would you do this to me! How could you take her from me? How can I explain this to her mentally ill mother? How? I've had enough!

David dropped his head in despair, and though Pastor Steve spoke, he heard nothing. The outpouring of support for David was astounding. The attendance to the funeral was of record numbers. David didn't engage in conversation with anyone. He did not care for anyone's support. He was broken.

When the procession reached the cemetery, the rain began. David let it seep through him. He felt nothing. God had become his friend when he brought Chance into his life. God gave him guidance on building the inn. God brought Marie into his life and blessed him with a wonderful family. God gave him wisdom and hope to offer others dealing with mental health issues. God gave him love for his wife regardless of her state of mind. God had been his confidante through all. God killed his baby girl. Who could he turn to now?

Marie's psychologist had spoken to him at the church. He had approached him at the cemetery as well. It was all a fog. Her nurse had sought him out too and insisted he listen to her. They were worried. He really needed to reconnect with Marie, they were saying. She was slipping into trouble again. She wasn't doing well. She needed him to be there for her. She had lost a child too after all, they'd said.

David wasn't absorbing their words; he decided he didn't care. For some reason he just couldn't care. He saw Scott and Clara mourning for their grandchild, he couldn't face them. He was tired, tired of being the strength, tired of having the answers, tired of helping others. Where was his help when he needed it? Tears stung his eyes again. Where was his daughter?

David stayed in the apartment in Raleigh that night, bruised and broken. He paced the rooms, reliving memory after memory and sound after sound. Her laughter had been infectious, and her intelligence astounding. Her joy had been unmatched. She had been pure, simple, beautiful and kind. He climbed onto Abigail's bed, turned his face into her pillow and sobbed. He could smell her shampoo. It had been the last place she'd slept. He fell into a fitful sleep filled with anger and discontent.

In the early morning, he rose before the sun and got dressed, simply to end the night. He did not want to sleep. He was tortured by his thoughts. He was bitter and angry, and nothing he could do could separate him from this evil. He left the building and walked the city, reaching every distant corner he had never been to before. He sat on park benches beside strangers and felt content ignoring and being ignored by others. The heat of the sun as it rose didn't impress its warmth on him, because he felt his soul was too cold.

The ducks at the manmade pond weren't cute; they were annoying. He watched as children threw bits of bread to them and listened to their dull quacks. Dirty birds, he thought, nothing but a nuisance.

He walked and walked some more, never feeling hungry or caring about any of the things he so proudly had accomplished in his life. It didn't matter that he'd built up communities; it didn't matter that the businesses around him had a chance to thrive once more. Nothing mattered. He ignored memories as they threatened to tug at him. He had a daughter once. He had a wife once. They had both been whole at one time. It all seemed so foreign to him now.

"Sir, are you okay?"

David got up and moved on as this stranger looked oddly at him. He could sense the judgment from others now, and it was real and justified. Something he felt he could agree with, in fact. There was no goodness in the world. There was greed and fear. There was control and intimidation. He felt like he had been a pawn that only succeeded in delaying reality. What was reality after all? Perhaps mental illness wasn't illness at all. Perhaps theirs was the reality the rest of screwed-up society chose to disregard and attack.

He found his way back to the apartment building but hesitated at the front door. The doorman even turned the other way for the wickedness David was sure he was emitting. He turned, though, at that moment and saw the transition house looming in front of him, and something tugged at his heart.

It was late in the day now. He sat down on the lawn as the sun was setting and looked up at the building he had worked so hard to establish, and rather than see himself in it, he suddenly saw his wife in it. In a moment, his heart softened, and he looked at this tragedy in his life as something she might be struggling with as well. How could he face her now?

Oh my God, what have I done? What is my wife going through? Is she hurting while I choose not to be there for her? Is she sedated once more? I don't even know how we could begin again without Abigail. Lord, please help me! Help me to be whole once more!

He stood and wavered while emotion coursed through him. The lights of the building came on as the darkness spilled in around him. He made steps toward the transition home his wife occupied. She had come so far. If it hadn't been for his selfishness, they would have been heading home as a family already. A family. His heart became heavy once more as he remembered their loss.

As David staggered slowly across the lawn leading to the marble stairs, he thought of the walks he and Marie had made across this same stretch of grass. He remembered the laughter, which always sounded filled with joy. He wondered how he could face her now.

He heard the door open and looked up at the top of the steps to see Marie's psychologist stepping through the doorway. David stopped and watched as he came down the steps and walked toward him.

"David, we have to talk."

"I know, I'm sorry," David said, "I've been having a really bad time. I know Marie's struggling. I'm sorry. Please understand."

"David, Marie knew that Abigail died."

"I know, I know," David interrupted. "I know I should've been here. You told me she needed me."

"David, you don't understand," he insisted.

"I didn't, but I do now. I'm here. I'm sorry."

"David, she's not here."

David was taken aback and stood firmly for a moment, confused, before realizing she must have been returned to the state hospital. He felt badly. He had not considered that anything might cause her, or them, to go backward in their progress to that degree. "Doctor, I..." David's voice trailed off as the guilt of his inattentiveness hit him.

"David, you don't understand."

David looked at the doctor as he completed what he needed to say.

"She believed that her illness, or the same illness, caused the death of your daughter. David, Marie committed suicide, they found her this morning."

David's legs wavered, then buckled. He crumpled to the ground in deep fits of sobbing. His heart was screaming out in anguish as he begged for freedom from this chasm of darkness.

No, Lord! Please don't do this. Please don't take Marie from me too. Oh my God, how can I live?

The sobbing overtook him, and no attempts by the doctor to try and get him to his feet could bring him up from this gloom.

No, no. Marie, Marie. I'm sorry! Please, no!

His mind was lost, and with tears distorting his vision, he looked upward out of his despair, and there she was. He took a breath and rubbed his eyes to fix his view. She was still there. He felt a glimmer of hope in his heart, and a race of excitement entered him.

"Marie?"

She stepped forward and reached out to touch him. "Yes, my dear. I'm here."

He felt the doctor walk away, leaving him alone with her. "Marie. Oh my God, I thought I'd lost you."

"I'm here, David."

EPILOGUE

He felt peace fill him at the sight of Marie, and joy replaced the deep sadness he had been consumed with. There was hope now, which he thought was gone, when suddenly the vision of her disappeared. He quickly stood, reaching out for her. He called her name, but she did not answer. In his heart, he became aware, deeply aware of the affects visions had on Marie, Abigail and other mentally ill people. They were real to them, as real as she'd just been to him.

He woke then in Abigail's bed. Confusion filled his head as he tried to make sense of what he had just experienced. What was real, and what was dream? He was having difficulty deciphering.

David, you have judged and condemned your loved ones' illnesses as if they were causing you some degree of suffering. Have you not just experienced the peace and familiarity such visions, such apparitions can bring? Seek to accept and continue to love. Love unconditionally as I have loved you. Go, share the compassion I taught you with your wife. Now, he was hearing things as well, God's voice, and it was loud and clear.

As the fog lifted from his mind, he sat up. He had been filled with so much anger over the loss of his child. He blamed the illness for taking her away. No, he blamed God. He had blamed the illness for changing his family, for altering his marriage, for taking away the normalcy of his wife, for taking away his freedom.

There was so much he had accomplished that was good in the face of these events, but those good deeds had become his identity. He was slipping further away from his intended role of husband and was seeking value in the opinions of others.

He arose from his little girl's bed and stepped to her doorway. It was time. Time for him to care for his wife as God had asked him to. He closed Abigail's door.

Thank you, Lord, for the time I had with her. She was a very special little girl.

After David showered and washed away the remainder of his anger and pride he, in humbleness, stepped out of the apartment building and walked to the open market two blocks away. When he returned, he was carrying a large bouquet of red roses and yellow daffodils.

He ascended the stairs of the transition house, determined to remind his wife what he had told her at Marie's Watch; if he could, he would marry her all over again. He stepped through the door Derek held open for him and, equipped with Christ's love and compassion, went inside to help Marie cope with the loss of their daughter.

Lightning Source UK Ltd.
Milton Keynes UK
UKOW07f2203141214

243121UK00015B/183/P